# Snowman

Book Four in the *Beach Reading* Series

Praise for the *Beach Reading* series

"If you've ever searched desperately for a fun, readable book to slip in your back pocket before heading out, take note—Mark Abramson has been there. [His] desire to discover the next Armistead Maupin led him to begin his own locally set queer series. He called it 'Beach Reading' to describe the kind of fiction he was seeking—entertaining, lighthearted and just a little bit trashy."

Louis Peitzman, *San Francisco Chronicle*

"Mark Abramson's love for San Francisco is most evident in his 'Beach Reading' series; a gay valentine to the City by the Bay that promises to be the best book series of its kind since Armistead Maupin's *Tales of the City*."

Jesse Monteagudo, *AfterElton.com*

"Abramson paints a wonderful picture of the diverse yet cohesive, supportive Castro community, and I can't wait until his next book to take me back to them."

Bob Lind, *Echo Magazine*

"Abramson is quite a writer. His characters are drawn beautifully and his plot... is carefully thought out. He pulls us in and does not let go even after we close the book. Not many can do that to me."

Amos Lassen, *amazon.com*

"Bret Harte—the writer, not the wrestler—helped found the literary convention of local color while living on the California coast. 150 years later, Mark Abramson—the writer, not the producer—makes his own contribution to that rich tradition by applying his verbal pointillé to San Francisco. In this first novel of an upcoming series, lovelorn Tim Snow becomes collateral damage after the collision of politics and partying... and love's rôle in both. Clever and sexy with a ton of heart (and Harte)."

—*Instinct Magazine*

# SNOWMAN

Also by Mark Abramson

*Beach Reading*

*Cold Serial Murder*

*Russian River Rat*

# Snowman

Book 4
in the
Beach Reading Series

Mark Abramson

Lethe Press
Maple Shade, NJ

Printed in the United States of America
Book Design by Toby Johnson
Author Photograph: David K. Bruner davidkbruner.com

*Acknowledgements*

*I would like to thank my favorite Gemini twins, Brian Heinen and Kegan Daniels, for their keen eyes, sound judgments and loving support during the process of bringing this book to its final form.*

*Mark Abramson*
*San Francisco*
*May 25, 2010*

Published as a trade paperback original
by Lethe Press, 118 Heritage Avenue, Maple Shade, NJ 08052.

ISBN 1-59021-142-1 ISBN-13 978-1-59021-142-7

Despite any resemblance to living and / or historical figures, all characters appearing or mentioned in *Snowman* are fictional except: Harvey Milk, David Weissman, Liam Neeson, Wolfgang Amadeus Mozart, Her Royal Majesty, Empress of San Francisco, José I, The Widow Norton, Laura Linney, Anita Bryant, Lady Gaga, Sarah Palin, The Kinsey Sicks, Rachel Maddow, Bill Cosby, Carol Channing, Mort Sahl, Julie Andrews, RuPaul, Bette Davis, Alfred Kinsey, Al Parker, Donna Sachet, Pyotr Ilyich Tchaikovsky, Nancy Kwan, Liberace, Vidal Sassoon, Betty Ford, Chris Isaak, Barbra Streisand, President Barack Obama, SF Chronicle columnist Leah Garchik, San Francisco Supervisor and 2011 Mayoral Candidate Bevan Dufty, Billie Holiday, former Supreme Allied Commander General Wesley Clark and Thomas Kinkade.

# Chapter 1

That warm spring morning in San Francisco, any passerby on Hancock Street might have heard Tim Snow scream, not a very butch scream, as he slid down his front stairs. He swore when he hit the bottom. After spending much of the winter confined to bed, Tim consoled himself that he still had enough flesh on his butt to cushion the landing.

Tim's downstairs tenant Jane Larson leaned out her front door. "What are you doing? You shouldn't try to take those stairs by yourself. Where's Nick? Why isn't he helping you?"

"I'll be fine in a minute." Tim scowled, but he didn't attempt to move. He felt his right ankle starting to swell and rubbed it a while until he had to admit it was only his overactive imagination. "I need to learn to manage for myself." He paused, then offered her a smile, "Well, one favor. Would you hand me the mail?"

Jane flipped open the lids on both mailboxes. "None yet."

"I thought I heard footsteps on the sidewalk and someone banging around down here."

"You probably heard the garbage truck or the kids across the street."

"Must have been the neighbors' brats." Tim had long ago decided that kids were cute until they hit eleven and then were best left unseen until a decade after puberty. "Where are your kids?"

"Sarah's eating breakfast and the baby is asleep."

Tim gave Sarah extra-allowance because she was honestly sweet-natured. "I've hardly seen the magic child all winter."

"She asks about you all the time, but I tell her Uncle Tim needs his rest. Come on, can I help you up?"

"Nah, it's such a nice day I think I'll just sit here and wait for the mailman. He's been coming about this time every morning lately. Invalids notice such things."

Jane groaned at his melodramatic quip. "Expecting him to deliver a walker?"

"No... Everyone gave me subscriptions last Christmas. How many copies of *Inches* does a guy need? I should just donate them to the doctor's office waiting room."

"Only in San Francisco could you get away with that."

"Do you know what drives me crazy? Dolores Park is right there at the end of our street. I miss walking it so much."

"I heard they're talking about closing it for a couple of years."

"What? They couldn't."

"New landscaping, new playground, new restrooms. Better enjoy it while we can."

"Even on a sunny day like this I don't think I could walk over there and back, at least not without stopping to rest. When we lived on Collingwood I used to lace up my sneakers and jog over there and run laps around the park like it was nothing. Getting old is a drag."

Jane laughed. "You should spend nine months pregnant sometime. You're just feeling sorry for yourself, that's all. Come on. Get up. Let me help you." She gently pulled him to his feet. "Lean on me and we'll walk for awhile. Can you push a stroller? We could take the kids to the park?"

"A stroller is a lot like a walker, isn't it? You get the kids ready. I'll crawl back upstairs and get my house keys."

. . .

The walk seemed to do Tim good. Near the playground, they spread a blanket below the grassy shelves of the southwest corner, where so many gay men in the neighborhood sunbathe. Tim missed the feeling of the sun on his bare skin. Despite the fine weather, only a dozen or so people were in the park, but then it was still morning. As Sarah rushed for the nearby swings and Jane checked on her baby, Samuel, in the stroller, Tim eyed the men in the park.

He whispered to Jane, "Look at the guy in the black trunks… the one basted in suntan oil."

Jane whistled appreciatively. "He must spend all his free time at the gym. Do you know him?"

Tim chuckled. "Last summer I was at the pool up at the Triple R in Guerneville. And he was there…"

"Yeah?"

"I was just killing time waiting for Nick to finish work at the nursery and everybody was drooling over that guy. He obviously loves the attention. Then a friend must have waved and the guy yelled back. The moment that mouth flew open a pink gingham dress fell right out." Tim dropped back to the blanket and laughed.

"Tim, you're terrible!"

"It's sad, but true… they don't come any nellier than him… thank goodness."

Tim stared a while at the sky. He didn't want the light-heartedness to end. The solution to that was somewhere in his backpack. "Do you wanna smoke a joint?"

"No thanks. Ben and I have pretty much given it up when the kids are around, which is like… always. You go ahead."

"And that's why gay men shouldn't adopt."

"So… why haven't I been seeing Nick around?"

"What's that?" His fingers found the Altoids tin where he kept his favorite "medicine." *Oh, California,* he thought, *if you aren't going to let gays marry, you better vote in November to allow us to toke.*

"I thought he had pretty much moved in upstairs, but it's been ages since I've noticed his truck in the driveway."

"He's back up in Monte Rio. The place needs a good spring cleaning, and there's his new nursery outside Sebastopol. The insurance company finally settled on the damages from the fire, so he's rebuilding everything. Not by himself. I'm sure he's hired a swarm of hunky carpenters, electricians, glasscutters, plumbers..." Tim flicked the lighter and toasted the far end of the joint.

"Is everything okay between you two?"

Tim took his first hit of the day and gazed at the skyline of downtown San Francisco. So beautiful even without a bit of THC. He never grew tired of the view from Dolores Park. There might be higher hills in the city and more dramatic views, ones that included the Pacific Ocean or the Golden Gate Bridge, but this one felt like he owned it, as if it were his back yard.

"Nick and I..." The second hit off the joint made him cough. "I don't know. All winter long he took care of me. Honest, I felt guilty for what happened."

"For heaven's sake, it's not your fault. Nick knows *you* weren't the one who messed with the brakes on his truck."

Tim shrugged. "But he feels guilty that I ended up behind the wheel when that asshole intended to kill him. Does it matter who feels guilty?" Maybe the pot wasn't good stuff; his mood had begun to sour. "Some days I actually resented him being always there."

"Nick is good for you. Hell, you're good for each other."

"We've hardly had any sex life since before it happened. I was either drugged up or in pain and I'm sure Nick has lost all interest in my ass after having to wipe it for me all winter. No, not literally, but he would have. He's that good a guy." Tim reached into his bag for a bottle of water and took a deep swallow.

"I just don't think I was a big turn-on covered in plaster of Paris. He's always had his bondage fantasies, but they were more fun when I could pretend to fight back."

Jane waved a hand in front of her face as if it could ward off her laughter. "I'm sorry. It's such a visual. I'm picturing you encased in some golden sarcophagus like King Tut at the DeYoung Museum."

"Go ahead and laugh." Tim sighed and smiled. The sun was climbing the sky by now and the dew on the newly mown grass was dry. "There's no way they could close this park for two years."

"It's beautiful here, isn't it? Maybe it was just one of those plans they 'float' at a meeting and then they discuss it to death and it gets dropped. I don't know."

"I've been really boring lately, probably because I'm bored to death. I've read all the books Arturo loaned me and we've watched every one of those old VHS Bette Davis movies that Jason left in the store room. One night I drifted off watching *All About Eve* and woke up to Al Parker in *The Other Side of Aspen*. Jason must have taped over one or the other of them. It's gotten to the point where I pretend to fall asleep, just so Nick can switch over to porn and take care of himself while he thinks I'm dead to the world."

"I don't like the sound of this. You can't give up on what was once a very good thing."

"I think we need a break from each other. I'm not ready to go back to work at Arts yet, and the restaurant is doing fine without me. Aunt Ruth packs them in on her bartending shifts a couple of times a week… whenever Sam lets her out of his sight."

"My dad's crazy about her. I've never seen him so smitten with anyone. "

"Aunt Ruth doesn't have to say much about it, but I know her well enough that I can read between the lines. He makes her very happy and she deserves that after her rotten husband dumped her for a young trophy bride. I'm pretty sure I can drive my car now and thanks to you I've proven that I can walk again. I've been thinking about taking a nice long drive along the coast, if my doctor says it's okay. Nick bought a new truck to replace the one that was wrapped around a tree with me inside it, so he doesn't need my car anymore."

"Where will you go? Up north?"

"No. Nick is north. I'll go south. Just put the top down on Jason's old Thunderbird and head down Highway 1. Maybe I'll see if my old friends in L.A. still remember me. Or I'll drive down to Laguna Beach and check into one of those little gay resorts beside the ocean." Tim held up one arm. "This pasty flesh needs some sun."

"And you can eat overpriced shrimp cocktails and stroll on the beach and drink beer and Margaritas and stare at the beautiful boys."

Tim smirked. "Nothing wrong with staring at Speedo tan lines."

"Are you planning on telling Nick that you're taking a vacation?"

Tim shrugged. "I guess so... not that he'd care very much. Maybe I'll send him an e-mail and see if he bothers to respond."

"I think what's really the matter is you're just feeling sorry for yourself. It's not like you and it doesn't become you."

"Sorry, Jane. You happened to catch me on the day I needed a girlfriend to confide in."

"Well, I'm always happy to do that for you. How long do you think you'll be gone?"

"I don't know." Tim stared across the park again for a long time, watching a pair of dogs chase a squirrel up the hill and bark at the base of an old Magnolia tree. "I think Nick needs some time alone so that he can miss me again. Don't worry. In the words of our illustrious governor, 'I'll be back.'"

# Chapter 2

On Thursday afternoon, Tim visited his physician, Dr. Hamamoto, for the okay to go on a road trip.

"I've been fine. Really. I started walking to Dolores Park and back nearly every day this week."

Hamamoto smiled. "Good for you, Tim. Walking is great exercise." Tim had actually seen his doctor jogging a couple times in the neighborhood. He had no idea if the man was gay or not—and didn't dare ask.

"Getting out of town might even be good for your head, but I don't like the idea of your going alone. What about that friend of yours who came along on your last few visits?"

"Nick's busy with his own life, but I'll be okay. He bought me a cell phone for Christmas. If I need anything, I can call."

"Program my number into that cell phone."

"I promise."

Hamamoto then went over his latest blood results and instructed Tim that when he returned to the city, he'd have to go back on the retroviral drugs. The news wasn't unexpected. His HIV drug "vacation" should have been up at Christmas, but with him laid up for most of the winter, his doctor had extended the break. But the test showed that his T-cell count was dropping and his viral load was detectable again. Tim had reacted to the protease inhibitor "cocktail" very well the last time. He wasn't worried.

The next morning Tim made himself scrambled eggs, toast and coffee. As he showered, he daydreamed about the ride down the highway. As a kid, he always liked long drives. He suddenly remembered one of the best, a trip he made with his grandmother years and years ago, to some out-of-the-way ice cream stand that served the best sundaes. She had treated the trip as if it were a grand hunting expedition, but instead of bagging a lion or tiger it would be hot fudge and bananas.

Out of the shower and wrapped in a towel, he went to his bedside table, where he kept the framed photograph of his grandmother and him. She sat with her arm around him on a blue and green plaid blanket beside the lake in Powderhorn Park in Minneapolis. It was the Fourth of July, and they were waiting to hear the Symphony play *The 1812 Overture* and the fireworks to begin. Tim had on red swim trunks and he was holding a tiny American flag.

Tim smiled. The woman had shared more than love with him; he'd inherited her knack for psychic dreams.

He started packing for the trip, a bit of everything in case the weather changed fast, then he realized he was over-packing. "Oh well, that's every gay man's prerogative," Tim said to himself.

The last thing Tim packed was the other framed photograph from the bedside table. A picture of Nick and Tim arm-in-arm beside the pool at the Triple R Resort. Tim placed the picture face down on top of the soft stack of multicolored t-shirts and tank-tops in his bag and zipped it shut.

Tim couldn't leave the city without first saying goodbye to his Aunt Ruth. So he drove to her apartment on Collingwood. He decided to block the driveway for a few minutes, rather than try to find parking. As Tim got out of the car, Teresa opened the gate to retrieve her morning paper. "Tim, it's good to see you up and about!" She held the gate for him. "How are you getting along without the crutches? Where's Nick?"

"Up north getting the nursery back up and running after the fire." *Why did people always ask about Nick?* He started to feel like he was expected to be joined at the hip with the man. "Is Aunt Ruth awake yet?"

"I don't know, honey. I haven't seen her in a few days."

Tim still had a set of keys to the gate and to Ruth's front door. The apartment had been his for years until he inherited Jason's house on Hancock Street. Aunt Ruth insisted that he keep a set of keys. "...just in case," she said.

*In case of what?* Tim had never dared to ask, but it seemed to comfort her to know that he had them. And it seemed like a good idea for Ruth to have a set of keys to his house on Hancock Street, too.

Ruth didn't answer his first or second knock, but he didn't see any reason to go inside. He'd call her from whatever motel or resort he ended up staying for the night.

He heard footsteps from the staircase where Teresa had headed and looked up to see Artie coming down.

Artie was co-owner with his partner Arturo of Arts restaurant on Castro Street. Since Tim worked there as a waiter, and Aunt Ruth had become the neighborhood favorite fixture behind the bar, the men felt like family rather than Tim's bosses.

"Hello, Timmy! Teresa said she let you in. Let me get a good look at you, dear boy. How are you?" Artie enveloped Tim in a deep hug.

"Hey, Artie, I'm fine."

"You're as pale as a ghost and you must have lost twenty pounds! Isn't Nick feeding you these days? Why didn't you let us know? Arturo could send over a plate of food from the restaurant every night. We'll start today! We can fatten you up again, Darlin'."

"I'm fine. Honest. You're the one who's lost weight. I knew you were dieting, but now it really shows."

"God love you, boy. You remember how I got into my red outfit for the Christmas party?"

Tim nodded and smiled at the memory of Mrs. Santa Claus. Artie had surprised everyone by reviving his old drag persona Artie Glamóur from his glory days at Finocchios nightclub in North Beach.

"I realized how much I'd missed the audience and the applause. And then I thought of all the gorgeous gowns I have in storage because I couldn't fit into them anymore without a shoehorn." Artie sighed. "Well, I just decided things had gotten out of control."

"You were great, Artie. I had no idea you could really sing."

"Only in character, though. When I put on a face and a wig and a dress I am transformed. I become someone else, some fabulous illusion of my own creation who can do things that this old fart you're looking at now would never dare try. Well, anyway… I took three of my favorite old beaded gowns out of mothballs. I hung up one in the kitchen at the restaurant, one beside the refrigerator here at home, and one next to the scale in the bathroom. There is no motivation like an old queen's vanity. I'm determined to take my pick between those three dresses by next Halloween – maybe in time for Pride in June."

"Good for you, Artie. I think you should run for Empress or something."

"If I wasn't so old, I would, but that's a lot of work and time and travel. Leave all that for the younger ones. I wanted to run years ago, but Arturo wouldn't hear of it. He said going from Artie Glamóur to mere San Francisco royalty would be a step down, but I don't know… I always thought it might be fun. Those were the days when they'd have a whole bunch of candidates every year—it all started here in San Francisco, you know, with the Widow Norton, Jose Sarria—but nowadays they seem to have trouble getting anyone to take the job. Ah… so many things have changed, you know…"

"I'm sure they have..." Tim was glad to see Artie so enthusiastic about losing weight, but he didn't want to be stuck here all day listening to tales of the old days at Finocchios or the way the Castro used to be. When Artie got wound up, he could talk forever! "Hey, I just stopped by to see if my Aunt Ruth was home."

"You're the second one this morning," Artie said with a scowl.

"Second one what? What do you mean?"

"Some gal was here about half an hour ago, rang all the doorbells in the building and raised quite a ruckus. She parked right here where you are and she had to move her car to let Arturo out. He likes to shop early in the morning, you know," Artie's smile returned. "She didn't like that one bit. She had a big fancy rented town car and she was already acting all flustered when she got here, probably wasn't used to the hills or the narrow streets. As soon as Arturo left, she pulled right back in and started yelling up at me again. I told her to pipe down. The nerve of her, ringing everyone's doorbells at that hour! You'd have thought I had Ruth held captive or something."

"What did she look like?"

"She was about your age, I guess, maybe a few years older. She had on an expensive suit and good jewelry – believe me, I can tell the difference from paste a mile away. She wore a little too much make-up and her hair was sprayed to death. She could have ridden a float through a wind tunnel and come out the other end looking none the worse for wear. Her wrist might have got tired from waving it against the wind, I suppose, but she didn't look the type that would ever let that stop her. That's it!"

"What's it?"

"That's what she reminded me of – a beauty queen!" Artie said with a snap of his fingers. "She was a real bitch, too—pardon my French—like Anita Bryant or Sarah Palin. They're both from the same school. I'll bet you anything this broad this morning had been in a pageant or two when she was younger... lots younger. Some gals get hooked on the tiaras and they never outgrow that sort of thing. They're worse than drag queens, if you ask me."

"So... you said she was asking for Aunt Ruth, too? What did you tell her?"

"I flat-out lied and told her I didn't know where Ruth was. Pardon me, but I didn't like the way she asked, so I lied! I didn't think it was any of her business where Ruth was, especially after she woke up the whole building. You know the new boys, Tony and Jeff on the second floor. They like to go out dancing on Friday nights and I'm sure they don't appreciate any noise before noon on a Saturday. She didn't care, anyway. She said she had Ruth's cell phone number and she'd track her down sooner or later without any help from me."

"So you lied..." Tim said.

"So, sue me... I didn't like the bitch, if you'll pardon my French again, and I don't mean to give pregnant canines a bad name, either—"

"Artie!" Tim interrupted. "If you lied, that means you *do* know where my Aunt Ruth is. Aren't you going to tell *me*?"

"Oh... right... sorry..." Artie sat down on the stairs. "She's not here. In fact, she asked me to water your little old garden outside the back door, which I gave a good soaking to on Wednesday. Let's see, it was Sunday when she left. She worked Friday and Saturday nights behind the bar with Scott and then she worked Sunday brunch with me. It slowed down enough by about 2:30 that she asked if she could go early and I said sure. I could handle it alone. That's when she asked me to water the plants for her and..."

"Where the hell did she go? Where is she now?"

"She's with Sam, of course. She's at his place down in Hillsborough right now, I imagine. She's been spending most of her days off down there all winter." Artie looked up at Tim and asked, "What do you mean? Didn't *you* know?"

"I guess not, Artie," Tim admitted. "I've had Nick staying with me all winter and I've only talked to my Aunt Ruth on the phone every week or so."

"She's mentioned that to me a couple of times..." Artie looked Tim straight in the eye as his words trailed off.

"Mentioned what?"

When Artie was sure that Tim was paying full attention, he went on. "She mentioned how glad she was that Nick was there to take care of you and that you didn't seem to need her so much lately, but she felt like maybe Sam needed her a little more these days."

"What's wrong with Sam?"

"Nothing is wrong with Sam, you ninny! The point is that your Aunt Ruth is happy for you and Nick, but you might let her know that you're thinking about her too, now and then. You might let her know that you still need her, at least a little bit."

"Well, Artie... the reason I came by right now was to see her and get caught up on everything before I leave town."

"Leave town." Artie shrieked. "What do you mean? Where do you think you're going? Arturo will be devastated. What about Nick? What are you talking about, leaving town?"

"I'm not leaving town for good, Artie, just taking a little drive. Nick is busy getting the nursery back together and I thought I might go down to L.A. and look up some old friends. They were really friends of Jason's, but when they came up for his memorial service they said I should come and visit anytime. Do you think they meant it?"

"Well, maybe... I don't know. People always say those things, but do they ever really mean them? There's only one way to find out, but I'd at least call them first. If they don't welcome you with open arms, you could always check into the Coral Sands, I guess." Artie winked at him. "I won't tell anyone."

"I've heard some pretty wild stories about that place." Tim grinned. "Well, I just thought I'd head down the coast highway and take my time, free as a bird. Since Aunt Ruth's not here, maybe I'll stop off in Hillsborough first and surprise her. You don't happen to have Sam's address, do you?"

"There's a good boy," Artie said with a smile as he hoisted himself off the steps into a standing position again. "Of course I do. She even drew me a map. We can make a copy of it, if I can figure out how to use Arturo's fax machine. Come upstairs with me and I'll find it for you right now."

# Chapter 3

It was just past 10:30 on Saturday morning when Tim pulled his red Thunderbird through the gates of Sam Connor's Hillsborough estate. Aunt Ruth's meticulously handwritten directions were easy to follow, considering this was Tim's first trip here. He couldn't remember having driven anywhere south of San Francisco before, except for the airport and a few stoned sunny afternoon trips with Jason to the gay ends of the nude beaches at Devil's Slide and San Gregorio.

Tim pulled up beside a large black town car and figured this must be the one Artie had mentioned, the nasty woman who'd stopped on Collingwood earlier and been so rude to him. The front door of Sam's house stood wide open and Tim heard women's voices talking inside. "Couldn't you at least get Delilah to bring my luggage in from the car?"

"Her name is Delia, not Delilah!" That was Aunt Ruth's voice and she didn't sound happy. "I've already told you her name twice, Dianne."

"Well, for heaven's sake! What-*ever*, Mother!" Now Tim recognized the whiny voice of his cousin Dianne, a former Minnesota girl transplanted to Texas. She was his Uncle Dan and Aunt Ruth's only child. Tim slunk down in the seat as far as he could and wondered whether he'd be able to start the engine and hit the road again before they noticed him.

"Furthermore, Delia is Sam's cook and head house-keeper and she's very good at what she does!" That was Ruth's voice again. "But her job does not involve schlepping your suitcases and hat-boxes around."

"Oh, Mother... where I come from the help is the help. I can't carry all those in the house by myself."

"How long did you plan to be away from home, anyway? How much luggage do you need to bring inside? You're welcome to freshen up, but this isn't *my* home. You don't think you can invite yourself to stay here at Sam's, do you?"

The two women appeared at the top of the marble front staircase now and Tim turned the key in the ignition, but the engine failed to catch. "Tim!" His Aunt Ruth had spotted him. "Thank goodness you're here. You remember your cousin Dianne," Ruth came running down the steps, across the driveway and toward his car.

Tim remembered his cousin Dianne, alright. He hadn't seen her in years, but he could hardly forget her. She was older now, of course, and even more scary-looking. Artie had been right about the lacquered hair and heavy make-up and in broad daylight, no less. Tim still pictured her in knee socks and black patent leather Mary Jane's, stomping down a flight of stairs by jumping on each step, as if she wanted to prove she was the boss. She always chewed gum like she was mad at it. Even then she was selfish, petty, mean—the opposite of her mother.

Tim thought back to his own mother, for some reason. She and his Aunt Ruth were each other's only siblings and they were polar opposites too, but in a different way. How many opposites could a person have? Tim remembered when he was very small, when his mother still held down a job and drank on weekends. She would drop him off at the neighbor lady's house or at his grandmother's or else his Aunt Ruth would come and pick him up with Dianne strapped into the passenger seat so Tim would have to sit alone in the back. He could swear that he never saw the world from the front seat of a car until he was old enough to learn how to drive one.

Aunt Ruth and Uncle Dan lived in Edina, where Dianne had long outgrown the tree house Tim loved. Or it wasn't "ladylike" enough for her. Maybe that was it. She hated getting dirty, which was something Tim didn't mind, even nowadays. He would climb up there and read all afternoon, but that must have been later. His memory played tricks on him.

Tim gave up on starting the engine and got out of the car to give his aunt a hug as his dear old Cousin Dianne approached. Tim was unsure of what to do next, but he stepped forward and extended his right hand. She jerked her own hands behind her back and said, "He's awfully pale. Does he have AIDS?"

Tim's jaw dropped, but he managed to turn to his Aunt Ruth and say, "Since we're communicating in the third person, please tell my cousin Dianne how nice it is to see her, too. She's looking well for her age – not a day over fifty, I'd say… but my, what big hair!"

"Fifty!" Dianne screamed. "I'm nowhere near fifty. I'm nowhere near forty yet!"

"Stop it!" Ruth said. "…both of you!" She took Tim by the hand and led him inside the house, leaving her daughter outside with the front door wide open. "If Sam heard this kind of talk, he'd throw all three of us out and I can't say I'd blame him one bit."

Sam rounded the corner into the front hallway in time to hear Ruth's last remark. "What kind of talk is that, dear? Oh! Hello, Tim. What a nice surprise. It's good to see you up and walking. How are you getting along? Where is Nick?

Tim shook hands with Sam. "Nick had to go back up north to get to work on the new nursery."

"He'll have to come down another time when he's not so busy. I'm sure the two of you boys would enjoy the pool and the tennis courts. The stables are just over there beyond the garage. You could go riding—"

Ruth laid a hand on Sam's arm. "My daughter Dianne is here too, I'm afraid—quite unexpectedly."

"Why, that's wonderful news, Ruth," Sam beamed. "You must be very happy to see her. Where is she?"

"She's right over..." Ruth turned toward the open door. "Well, she was right here a minute ago."

The three of them walked to the entrance and looked out to see Dianne at the back of her rental car, wrestling some enormous pieces of luggage out of the depths of the trunk. "I didn't invite her to stay, Sam, honestly..."

"Don't be silly, Ruth. Of course she can stay and Tim, too. We have plenty of empty bedrooms."

"Not me," Tim said. "Thanks, Sam, but there's no way. Some other time, maybe... I just stopped by to say hello and good-bye to my Aunt Ruth."

"What do you mean by good-bye?" Ruth asked. "Where on earth are you going?"

"I'm just going for a drive for a few days. Don't worry. I'm coming back again. I thought I might drive down the coast and visit some old friends in L.A. Or I might get tired of driving and stop somewhere along the way."

"Well, nobody's going anywhere without lunch, are they?" Sam said. "Ruth, would you ask Delia to set a couple more places at the table on the south terrace? I think it will be plenty warm enough to eat outdoors beside the pool, don't you? Tim, if you're up for it, maybe you could help me with your cousin's luggage before she hurts herself."

Lunch was delicious, but far from relaxing. The terrace overlooked a swimming pool lined with padded deck chairs. At the far end, roses the size of salad plates covered a pair of latticework gazebos. Sam explained that one of them concealed a shower and changing room and on the other side was a Jacuzzi hot-tub that seated a dozen people "... so you and Nick should invite all your friends down here sometime and enjoy the amenities."

"That sounds great, Sam." Tim could imagine what kind of trouble all of his and Nick's friends could get into if they had the run of a place like this. Sam introduced Delia to Tim and Dianne, who refused to shake hands with the petite African-American woman. Tim thought his cousin was merely homophobic, but she was apparently a racist too.

"Delia has been with me for nearly thirty years," Sam said to no one in particular. "She's a treasure in the kitchen."

"I can attest to that." Ruth took a sip of her soup. "I have to watch myself or I'd be packing on the pounds every time I come to visit Sam."

"You don't need to worry, Ruth," Sam said. "You're in excellent shape and I'll help you stay that way with a game of tennis this afternoon, if you're willing – that is, unless Tim or your daughter want to challenge you first. Maybe we could play doubles?"

"I'm lousy at tennis," Tim said, "but the pool sure looks inviting."

"Swimming is wonderful exercise, Tim," Sam said. "It would do you good and some of Delia's home cooking couldn't hurt, either. You have room to put on a few pounds."

"I will in time," Tim agreed, "...especially now that I'm up and about. I've been walking to Dolores Park nearly every day, working up an appetite. Food was the last thing on my mind when I was holed up in bed all winter. By the way, this vichyssoise is great, Delia."

"My soup is cold!" Dianne grumbled under her breath, but just loudly enough for everyone to hear her.

"Vichyssoise is supposed to be served cold, dear," Ruth said.

"Well, I never..." Dianne pushed her plate away and stood up from the table.

"Thank you, Tim," Delia smiled, removed Dianne's full soup plate and disappeared into the house. She had put out quite a spread on the terrace's sideboard and left the foursome to fend for themselves. Dianne took a plate and helped herself to pasta salad, which was also unexpectedly cold to her, and several slices of assorted cheeses and meats. A wicker basket held homemade sandwich rolls in a linen napkin. They were fresh and hot from the oven and gave off the yeasty smell of an old-fashioned bakery.

Delia came out of the house again with a pitcher of iced tea. "Where is Frank this afternoon, Delia?" Sam asked, and then turned to explain to his guests. "Frank is Delia's husband. He takes care of the grounds and the stables. The two of them are the only members of the domestic staff who live here on the premises full-time."

Dianne paid no attention to Sam. She was too busy examining her cold cuts. Then she picked apart her pasta salad and set aside anything she didn't recognize.

Delia glanced at her wristwatch. "Frank should be on his way to the airport to pick up Adam. We haven't seen him since Christmas-time, you know."

"That's terrific, Delia," Sam said. "Tim can meet Adam. It might be nice for him to have someone closer to his own age around here."

"I'm closer to Tim's age," Dianne snapped. "But on second thought, I'm sure we have nothing in common."

Ruth tried to explain. "Dianne, I think what Sam meant was that it might be nice for Tim to have another young man around."

"Dianne," Tim said, "you might be surprised at how much you and I have in common. When I was a lot younger, I used to fool around with my hair color too, but that was years ago."

His cousin stopped picking at her food long enough to give him an icy stare.

"I stopped doing that in my early twenties, though. It always looked so phony. I like a more natural look, don't you? I guess not..."

"Are you insinuating something?" Dianne asked.

"Not at all, Dianne," Tim said and turned back to the others. "Aunt Ruth, did I tell you I finally finished that big box of old gay novels Arturo loaned me? There were some that went back to the 1970s – way before I was even born. And then Artie gave me this new one about a homicidal drag queen whose vanity is only surpassed by the true shallowness of her character. It's pretty good. She reminded me of Sarah Palin." He took a sip of his iced tea and glared at Dianne, who was still picking apart her pasta salad. "I can't imagine what made me think of that right now. Maybe because Artie mentioned Sarah Palin just this morning."

"Maybe he'll loan the book to me when you're finished with it," Ruth said.

"I'm on the last chapter now." Tim looked at how the sun sparkled on the clear blue water of the pool. He wasn't in such a big hurry to head south, after all. If he could keep his snooty cousin out of his hair, he might even enjoy some time with his Aunt Ruth and her wealthy beau. And if Dianne got in his way, he could have fun teasing her. "I'll bet I could finish the book this afternoon while I'm here and leave it with you."

Ruth turned toward her daughter. "You still haven't told us what brings you to California. This is quite a surprise. I thought you told me a long time ago that you'd never leave Texas again."

"Can't I come to visit my own mother?"

"Of course you can, dear," Sam cut in, "but perhaps the two of you can discuss all of that later, after lunch. Delia told me she's made a chilled raspberry soufflé for dessert. Would anyone like coffee to go with it? I'll ask her to put some on now."

"I'd love a cup," Tim said.

"Me, too," said Ruth. "Would you like a cup of coffee, Dianne?"

Dianne couldn't decide about coffee, one way or another, but she got herself another roll and some more cheese, apparently glad for any change of subject that didn't involve her hair color or make-up or some trashy gay novels that didn't interest her in the least.

# Chapter 4

It was Sunday morning when Nick Musgrove packed up a few things and got ready to drive down to the city. It didn't take him nearly as long to pack as it took Tim. It didn't take Nick nearly as long to do anything. He didn't fuss about what to wear or what he might want to wear later. Clothes were clothes. He knew how to dress comfortably for most situations without having to think much about what to pack. Nick was a practical man, Tim's opposite in many regards.

He missed Tim terribly. Even after all the years of living alone, this winter he'd grown spoiled by waking up beside Tim every morning in San Francisco. Nick looked around the bedroom of his little house in Monte Rio and his eyes landed on the photograph of the two of them beside the pool on a perfect afternoon at the Triple-R Resort last summer. Nick blew the dust off the chrome frame and smiled. The cleaning lady would come on Monday afternoon, but Nick knew that if Tim were here, he would have kept the dust off it.

This whole business of taking a break from each other was Tim's idea. Nick just went along with it... sort of. It was Tim who thought they needed time apart, now that he could take care of himself again. Now it had been a full week since they'd seen each other. This was the longest time they'd gone without even speaking since Tim was in a coma after the "accident" with Nick's truck last winter. A week was more than enough, in Nick's opinion. Too much!

Tim told Nick he should get back to work and rebuild the nursery. When the insurance money came through, Nick realized he could make the place exactly how he'd always dreamed it should be. He'd tried to fill the hours by making plans and dealing with contractors, but without Tim around his heart wasn't in it.

Nick stretched his long limbs and put the coffee on. By the time he finished his shower it was ready and so was Nick. He threw a few things in a bag, poured the fresh pot of coffee into a Thermos, grabbed the keys to his new truck and hit the road. The coffee was gone before the Golden Gate Bridge came into view.

Tim's downstairs tenants, Ben and Jane Larson's blue Volvo stood in the driveway on Hancock Street, but there was no sign of Tim's Thunderbird. Nick thought maybe he'd gone grocery shopping which meant that he was at least well enough to be up and about. Nick pulled into the driveway and sat in his truck for a moment. He had a set of keys to Tim's flat, but it would feel strange using them when Tim wasn't home. It was one thing to let himself in as he had all winter when Tim was lying there waiting for him. This was different. Still, Nick needed to take a leak, so he decided… what the hell.

Leaving the apartment a couple of minutes later Nick glanced in at Tim's bedroom. His bed was neatly made and everything looked to be normal except that the picture in the chrome frame was missing. Nick could only wonder what that meant. He locked the door again and came down the front stairs.

"Are you back home already, Tim?" Nick heard Jane's voice from the downstairs flat. "I thought you'd be gone for a lot longer than just one night. What happened? …oh! Hello, Nick. I didn't think Tim could be back from his trip already. How are you?"

"Hi Jane... back from what trip? Did Tim say where he was going?"

"Well, I..." Jane tried to decide how much of what Tim had said was in confidence. "Won't you come in? How about a cup of coffee?"

"No thanks, I drank a whole Thermos-full on the way down here this morning."

"Come in anyway. Sit down. I'm having some. How about a danish?"

"Well, okay, I guess I could have one more cup of coffee, too..." Nick figured that if bad news was coming, he might want to be sitting down.

"Have you talked to Tim lately?" Jane pulled a cup and saucer down from the cupboard as Nick removed a doll from the nearest chair and sat down, still holding Raggedy Ann in his lap.

"No, not this week... he said he thought we needed a little break."

"Have you tried calling him?"

"Sure, I've tried. All I get is his answering machine. He never answers that new cell phone I bought him, either. It was just last week he started talking about us having some space. God, I hate that word! I don't feel like we need any *space* from each other." Nick took a sip of coffee and added cream. "What did he tell you?"

"He basically said the same thing, but he made it sound more like it was your idea. He said he was afraid of being a burden and he didn't want you to get sick of taking care of him and..."

"That's ridiculous! I love taking care of him. It makes me feel needed."

"Well, you know Tim," Jane offered a weak smile. "At least you know him a lot better than I do."

"I'm not so sure. Sometimes I think I do, until he says something silly like that. I would have been happy to push him down to City Hall in his wheelchair and get married if they were still granting licenses to gay couples. I could have sworn 'in sickness and in health' and all the rest of that stuff and I would have meant every word of it!"

"Why don't you and Tim get married anyway?" Jane asked. "You could elope to Iowa and then fly back and celebrate at the restaurant with all your friends and families. What a great excuse for a party."

"I think you've been living in the Castro too long, Jane."

"Arturo and Artie got married, you know, back during that little window of time when it was legal, but they hardly told anyone about it until later. They didn't want a big fuss, I guess."

"Tim and I have talked about a commitment ceremony, but you know how he is. He didn't want to do it while he was in a wheelchair. You know... for the sake of the pictures."

Jane laughed. "He's just as vain as he is paranoid."

"You know him better than you think. But where did he go on this trip? Did he tell you?"

"He said he wasn't sure where he was going, just that he needed to get away." Jane picked up her crying baby.

"Get away to where, I wonder?" Nick realized he was squeezing the doll so hard that one of her button eyes was about to pop off. He let go his tight grip, smoothed the doll's little dress and set her up on the table.

"Tim talked about taking a long drive down the coast... maybe L.A. Why don't you swing by Collingwood, Nick? Ask Tim's Aunt Ruth? I'll bet she would know. He wouldn't leave town without checking in with her first."

"Good idea. Thanks, Jane... and thanks for the coffee."

Nick pulled his truck onto Collingwood Street as a car vacated a handy parking spot near Arturo and Artie's building. The driver honked and waved. It was Teresa, Ruth's neighbor from the top floor. Nick was about to press Ruth's doorbell when Arturo arrived at the gate, out of breath. "Nick, you're just the man I needed to see."

Walk with me over to the restaurant. Artie threw his back out trying to lift a beer keg last night, so he's upstairs in bed with a heating pad and a bottle of Vicodin. Brunch is going to be busy today and Scott will have to tend bar by himself if I can't get a hold of Ruth. She's not due back until tomorrow night, but Scott had to close by himself last night, so I know he'll be tired."

"Where is Ruth? How do you know she's not home? I need to ask her if she knows where Tim is."

"She's been down at Sam's place in Hillsborough all week. Artie said Tim came by yesterday looking for her, too."

"Well, what do you need me for? I don't know anything about the bar business, except how to order a drink. I don't know how to make them."

"I didn't mean I wanted you to tend bar, Nick. I need a strong man with a good back, though. Late last night the toilet in the women's room backed up. I got hold of a plumber to come in, but it was two in the morning. I went home at 2:30 and left him there, still working. You can just about imagine what he's going to charge me for coming in at that hour."

"Did he get it fixed?"

"I sure hope so. He called when he was done and left a message that the snake wouldn't do it. They had to tear up the whole floor to get at the problem. The plumbing in that building is so old I'm sure it's pre-earthquake and I mean 1906 not '89. He said they had to tear up linoleum and tile and the sub-flooring under that, all the way from the toilet out to the back. The pipes were clogged in every direction, but they were the worst toward that old apartment building behind us on Hartford Street. I can't imagine how bad the place is going to smell this morning!"

Nick was fond of Tim's bosses, who were also Ruth's landlords, but he wasn't sure about getting involved in this mess at the restaurant that Arturo described. He just wanted to find out where Tim was and be on his way. "Sure, I'll help you," Nick heard his own words escape from his lips before he could stop them.

"I knew you would, and I promise I'll make it up to you, believe me."

. . .

Arturo turned on all the lights and the exhaust fans as soon as they set foot inside. He opened the windows and put two bar stools blocking the opened front door with the CLOSED sign to discourage any customers from thinking they were open.

"It doesn't smell so bad, Arturo,"

"I guess not... maybe a little. What do you really think, though... could you eat in here?"

"It hardly smells at all," Nick said. "I don't think anyone would notice it unless you told them, especially after we air it out good. Let's go look at the damage."

The bathrooms were located in the hallway between the swinging doors to the kitchen on the right and the stage on the left. The ladies' room door was still propped open and there was a pile of damp rubble and broken bits of tile and linoleum extending from the toilet bowl all the way down the hall to the emergency exit in the back of the building.

"Do you have a shovel? If not, I have some tools in my truck. I could walk back over to Collingwood and get them."

"There's a shovel in the closet off the kitchen," Arturo said. "And there should be some work gloves on the shelf inside the back door. Grab a pair for me, too. We can use those empty liquor boxes beside the dumpster; line them with heavy-duty trash-bags. I meant to have the busboy break them down last night, but I'm glad I let him go home. We all put in a big night."

Between Nick and Arturo, they filled several boxes with debris. Nick pulled his long blond hair away from his face into a ponytail and hoisted the heavy boxes onto his broad shoulders, one after another. He carried them out to the dumpster behind the restaurant.

Nick felt the sweat trickle down his back and he knew he would need another shower before he continued his search for Tim. He figured he could go back to Tim's apartment and let himself in again. He was used to Tim's shower by now—he even had his own toothbrush in the rack beside the bathroom sink—and this time he had an even better reason to let himself in when Tim wasn't home.

Nick threw box after box of debris over the side of the dumpster. "Aw… shit!" he yelled out loud when a black glob of something gelatinous landed on one of his shoes. This was not how he'd envisioned spending his Sunday morning in San Francisco.

"Are you alright?" Arturo yelled from inside.

"Yeah, I'm fine. You owe me a shoe shine, that's all."

Nick was glad to help out, but now he wished he had brought some work clothes with him. Maybe Tim was right when he packed for every occasion. This was a dirtier job than Nick ever imagined it would be. He hoisted another box of debris into the dumpster. He watched it break open and saw pieces of its contents slide down the pile of muck in slow motion. Nick gasped when he saw what looked like fingers of a human hand poking out at him.

"Arturo!" Nick yelled. "Arturo, you'd better come here. I think you need to have a look at something…"

# Chapter 5

Tim lounged beside the pool at Sam's Hillsborough estate with a mug of coffee in one hand and the current issue of Vanity Fair in the other. The cover promised an interview with Rachel Maddow on the inside. Tim loved her. He couldn't find the book he'd been reading about the killer drag queen and figured he must have forgotten it at home. It didn't really matter; he could finish it and get it to Aunt Ruth later.

The morning sun felt great on his pasty bare skin, but Tim still felt out of sorts. This wasn't what he had in mind when he left Hancock Street yesterday. He hadn't meant to spend the night here, but it was such a comfortable environment that it sucked him in. After lunch yesterday he'd had a swim and a nice visit with his Aunt Ruth and then there were afternoon poolside cocktails and last night Delia cooked them all a big dinner of bouillabaisse with crusty sourdough bread and lots of wine and he was in no shape to drive anywhere after that.

Tim set the magazine down, took a sip of coffee and closed his eyes. This was a far cry from his plan of hitting the open road with the top down on the Thunderbird. He yawned and rolled over to face the pool. Lying here in the sun was better than sitting home alone, anyway. He wondered how the work was coming along with the new greenhouses at Nick's nursery.

Tim reached for his backpack and his fingers found the Altoids box where he kept his pot. He hesitated for a minute and tried to hear if anyone else was stirring nearby. He didn't think anyone would mind if he smoked a little pot, just to take the edge off, but this was Sam's place, after all. Tim felt a little sneaky lighting the joint, took a couple of quick tokes before he snuffed it out on the grout between the tiles under his deck chair. Didn't anyone *have* ashtrays in California anymore?

Being stoned made him think of Nick, but Tim was determined to leave him alone for a while. Aunt Ruth always believed that old adage that absence makes the heart grow fonder. He hoped she was right. This afternoon, after lunch, Tim would leave Hillsborough, head over to the coast and then drive south on Highway 1. With a couple of hundred miles between them, he'd feel more secure about calling Nick. First he had to prove to everyone that he could get by on his own. He needed to convince himself as much as Nick that Timothy Snow didn't need anyone, no matter what his heart told him.

A tiny hummingbird, inches from Tim's face, hovered above a clay pot bursting with red geraniums. He could understand why Aunt Ruth loved spending time down here at Sam's. It was so quiet compared to the city, so much closer to the old suburban patterns of her married life in Edina than living in Tim's old apartment in the Castro. The smells of the earth and the vegetation—real living, growing things—reminded Tim of Minnesota summers when he was a child. Tim was stoned now.

He pictured himself staring out the back door of his parents' house, dirty laundry sorted in piles across the kitchen floor, his mother asleep on the couch by mid-morning. Tim was in diapers with his nose pressed against the screen door. He wanted to escape from the laundry smells to the green outdoors, but the hook was too high to unlatch, no matter how hard or how high he tried to jump. He reached down instead, inside his diaper, where his stubby fingers wrapped themselves around his stiff hairless prick. The little boy that

Tim was then already sensed he had his hand on something more important than he could understand. The smell of roses brought all of this back. The smell of roses growing up the side of the pool house in Hillsborough brought him back to that sea of green in Minneapolis years ago, his parents' back yard outside the screen door, just beyond his reach, the smell of summer coming on fast.

In those days his mother worked in the women's department of the old Sears store on Lake Street in south Minneapolis, the building that reminded him of a fortress or a castle surrounded by a moat of parked cars. She only drank on weekends then and always went to church on Sundays, no matter how poorly she felt. Even before she stopped working, the weekends started to get longer and run together, so his Aunt Ruth came to get him sometimes. It was later, when his parents found out about him and the track coach—the scandal that got him thrown out of their house—when he moved in with his Aunt Ruth and Uncle Dan full time. That was high school. Dianne had already grown up and moved out of their house by then.

Tim opened his eyes at the sound of birds in the treetops. He snapped back to California in the here and now, 2010. He heard a splash and someone swam towards him. Muscled brown arms climbed over the edge of the swimming pool and a handsome face popped up, smiled and shook the water off. "Good morning. You must be Tim."

"Hello," Tim said as he watched the stranger lift himself out of the pool in one smooth motion, a circus acrobat, a gymnast, a ballet dancer.

"Hi, I'm Adam. No... please... don't get up. But I think you're starting to burn. Don't you have any sunscreen?"

This young man was as stunning as the models in the magazine Tim had been mindlessly paging through earlier. His skin was the color of coffee with cream and he must be well over six feet tall.

Tim was alert now and he felt naked and ridiculous, so skinny and pale, but he couldn't help it; he'd been covered in casts and bandages most of the winter. He was determined to get back to the gym right after this trip, as soon as he returned to San Francisco. "There's some in my backpack, I think..." Tim reached for it. "You must be Frank and Delia's son, right?"

"Delia's," Adam corrected him. "My mother married Frank when I was a baby. He's a great guy, makes my mother happy."

"You don't look anything like Frank, come to think of it," Tim said. "My Aunt Ruth is Sam's..."

"Yeah, I know," Adam interrupted Tim before he needed to put a label on it. "I like her. She has kind eyes. You can tell a lot about a person by their eyes."

"The windows to the soul..."

"You and your Aunt Ruth are close, aren't you?"

"Yeah, we sure are. Sometimes we joke around that I should have been her son and my cousin Dianne should have belonged to my parents. When did you get here? I'm surprised I haven't seen you until now. I heard your mother say Frank was going to get you from the airport while we were having lunch yesterday."

"My flight was delayed in Chicago and then I missed my connection in Denver," Adam said. "I didn't get here until last night and we had a lot of catching up to do. Sam came by to say goodnight, but I stayed on the north side of the property. My mother and Frank live in that end of the house," he pointed. "I pretty much grew up there. Mom warned me about your cousin Dianne, too."

"Good thing... Where do you live now?"

"Manhattan, mostly... I work as a model, so I travel a lot. I just got back from Paris and Milan and then I took a week off in Chicago and now I have some free time to spend here."

"I thought you looked familiar," Tim said and pointed to the copy of Vanity Fair beside him. "Maybe I've seen your picture in a magazine."

"Not that issue, though. I was in last month's and before that last December. I'll be in next month's GQ, but I'm not in this one.

"Too bad," Tim said. "I would have asked you to autograph it."

Ruth was at the kitchen table with Sam, drinking coffee and discussing the events of the previous afternoon. "Sam, I can't thank you enough for being such a good sport about Dianne showing up here unexpectedly... and Tim too, of course."

"Ruth, you know Tim is always welcome here. I know how fond you two are of each another and I always enjoy his company. And in spite of your differences, Dianne is your daughter."

"I'm sure she wasn't counting on her cousin Tim showing up here to give her grief," Ruth laughed. "His timing couldn't have been better."

"At one point I was afraid they were going to push each other into the pool," Sam smiled and took Ruth's hand.

"Are you kidding? She wouldn't get near the pool. Can you imagine what it would do to her hair?"

"I wonder how she feels this morning. Don't you think you should go and check on her? She had quite a bit to drink last night."

"Let her sleep." Ruth shook her head. "I'm not going near her if she has a hangover. Besides, that girl has never willingly gotten out of bed before noon in her life!"

"This is California. We're on Pacific Time and her body clock must still be on—"

The phone rang on the counter and interrupted Sam's train of thought. Ruth was closer, so she picked it up. "Yes? Oh, hello, Arturo... Yes, this is Ruth."

She listened intently for a few moments as Sam watched the laughter leave her face. "Oh, my goodness, Arturo... and Poor Artie," she said. Sam moved around behind her chair and started to massage her shoulders as she talked.

"No, it's not a problem. I'll take a quick shower and get dressed and come straight away. I should be there within an hour if I can find parking. See you then. Good bye."

Sam replaced the phone in its cradle for her. "What happened? They need you to come in to work?"

"Yes, Artie threw his back out last night and Arturo said the plumbing went haywire… and they found something in the dumpster. He said he had to call the police, too… and then he wouldn't say another word. It sounds serious, but he said it would have to wait until he could tell me all about it in person. I'm so sorry. I know you were planning a barbecue this afternoon and it looks like a beautiful day for it, but they really need me."

"Don't worry about that," Sam said. "We can plan a barbecue for another time. Still, I wonder what we should do about Dianne."

"When she gets up—*if* she ever gets up—tell her something important came up at the restaurant and I had to go back to the city. If she could find me here in Hillsborough, she can find me in San Francisco. Besides, some exposure to the Castro would do her good. I'm sure they don't have the same kind of window displays in Houston or Dallas."

Sam smiled and shook his head. "I don't suppose they do. I was a little shocked the first time I took my granddaughter for a walk in the neighborhood. Nothing fazed her, of course. Tim is welcome to stay here as long as he likes, but what should I tell him about you? Do you want him to call you at the restaurant or what?"

"I'll talk to him before I go." Ruth gave Sam a kiss and ran out of the kitchen, showered, dressed and slid a tube of lipstick across her mouth. She dropped it into her purse at the same time she retrieved her car keys. Then she knocked at the door of the bedroom where Tim had spent the night, but there was no answer, so she continued to the end of the hallway and stepped onto the patio. "Tim, are you out here?"

Ruth rounded the corner to the pool and saw her nephew lying face down with a tall handsome man squatting over him. She thought at first that they were both naked, but the stranger wore brown swim trunks the color of his skin. The long fingers of his right hand rubbed oil into Tim's back and shoulders while his left hand rested at Tim's side. Now the fingers of both hands looked to be sliding under the waist band of Tim's swim shorts.

"Thanks, Adam," Tim said. "I shouldn't burn, now. Hey, Aunt Ruth! Come over here. You've met Adam, haven't you? He's Delia's son."

Adam wiped his oily right hand across his chest before he reached out to shake Ruth's. "Of course, we've met. How are you, Miss Taylor? It's good to see you again."

"Please call me Ruth..." she said and tried to remember their meeting, but it was too distracting to see him there on top of Tim, both of them with hardly any clothes on.

Adam stood and extricated his long limbs from physical contact with Tim's now well-oiled body. Ruth breathed a sigh of relief, even as he towered over her. "Are you going to come and join us for a swim?" he asked.

Ruth raised her hand to shield the sun from her eyes and thought she should also shield her eyes from Adam's near nakedness. She tried hard to picture him clothed, dressed as one of the boys on Castro Street, maybe—leather jacket, tight denim trousers and boots. That wasn't quite right. She tried to picture him in a suit and tie with dress shoes, a topcoat and maybe a pair of gloves. Now she remembered. They'd met in Paris. Sam spotted him at the airport when they arrived at Orly from London last winter. Sam greeted Adam like a long lost son. He introduced him to Ruth and said he was a model. Yes, he was beautifully dressed then and he chatted with Sam for a few moments until his flight was called. He said he was on his way back to California to see his mother after the holidays.

"No, Adam, I'm afraid I can't today. The pool looks inviting, but I just got a phone call from Arturo. Tim can tell you all about the restaurant. I have to head back to the city." Her gaze fell to Adam's large biceps and well-developed chest. He must spend every moment when he's not in front of the camera taking excellent care of himself.

"Is everything alright, Aunt Ruth?"

"Oh… you know Arturo. There's some kind of trouble at the restaurant, but when something is really upsetting him, he clams up. All I know for sure is that Artie threw his back out last night and they're desperate for me to come to work right away. I'll let you know if it's anything serious. He mentioned that the police were involved, so I'm curious. This might be a good time to stay out of the Castro, but I'd feel better if you were close by. Maybe you should spend a few days at the river instead of heading down south."

Tim gave her a stern look. "I already explained to you yesterday why I need to get away from there."

"Well, where is that cell phone that Nick bought you for Christmas?" Ruth thought that by saying Nick's name out loud it might dispel some of the sexual energy between her nephew and Adam.

"It's in the room where I slept last night. I left it plugged in to keep it charged up like I'm supposed to, but I haven't actually used it yet."

"Well, keep it with you and I can call you on it."

"Aw, okay. I'll stick it in my backpack in case of an emergency, like running out of gas or a flat tire, but neither of those is very likely. The gas gauge works fine and there's a spare tire and a jack in the trunk. I think I'm capable of changing a tire."

"I'm sure Nick would be relieved to know that you have the phone with you, too." There, she'd mentioned Nick's name again.

"I'll go get it in a little while."

"Have you told Adam about Nick?" Ruth asked. Three times might be the charm.

Adam laced his fingers together and raised his hands above his head to stretch. Ruth had a feeling that the crotch of his swim trunks was stretched as far as it could, too. She hoped he wasn't aroused from being crouched on top of Tim a moment ago.

"I'd better run along. It's nice to see you again, Adam. Be sure to keep that cell phone nearby, Tim, so I can call you. I'm sure Nick will be trying to call you, too." That was the fourth time she'd mentioned Nick's name. It was the best she could do.

Adam was stunning, Ruth had to admit, but she hated to see her nephew turn his back on everything that he and Nick had together. Well, it was out of her hands now. She had to get back to San Francisco and find out what the trouble at the restaurant was all about and there was no time to waste.

# Chapter 6

There were questions, questions, and more questions. The police cornered Arturo first, since he was one of the owners and he was also the person who'd made the call. Their interview with him seemed so endless and repetitive that he finally grew angry and told them he had better things to do. "Listen, Sunday brunch is supposed to start in an hour and I have prep work to do in the kitchen. I was afraid something like this would happen. I've told you all I know and I haven't even started on the hollandaise sauce. The plumber was here half the night and we'll have to sell a hell of a lot of Eggs Benedict to pay that bill!"

"We'll need to ask him some questions too, of course. Before you go back to the kitchen, please get us his name and number."

"If I'd known you were going to ask so many questions, I would have told Nick to keep his mouth shut about those fingers he found. We didn't have to call you, you know," Arturo kept complaining but he found the plumber's business card and set it down on the bar:

"Where did you find this guy?" Nick asked. "It sounds like he's advertising something besides plumbing. Does Phil work for him?"

"What do you mean? He was the only one whose advertisement said 24 hours. I found him in the back of this week's *B.A.R.*."

"With the hustler ads?"

"No, in the first section, back there with the goods and services." The paper was still beside the phone where Arturo had left it, folded to the page in question. Arturo drew a circle around the ad and tossed it on the bar next to the business card. "Here!" he said before he stormed back toward the kitchen.

Unlike most of the escort ads, the plumber didn't show his picture, Nick noticed. Now the interrogators turned their attention toward him. Up until this morning, Nick had never set foot inside Arts Bar and Restaurant unless Tim was there. But the police treated him as if he were intimately acquainted with the place. What was worse, the one who asked most of the questions made Nick feel like a suspect.

"I don't know anything," he pleaded. "I was just helping out Arturo. I don't work here."

"What is your relationship to the owners of this establishment?" the cop asked while he wrote in his notebook.

"None, I already told you."

"You just happened to be walking by on a Sunday morning, dressed in a Polo shirt, Bill Blass trousers, and a pair of expensive loafers?"

"Are they?" Nick looked down at his clothes, now streaked with dirt and grime from the chore of helping Arturo clean up the plumbing mess. How did this cop know so much about clothes? Nick had bought the shoes and slacks at Macy's in Santa Rosa. He remembered that the shoes were on sale that day and he could have sworn the trousers were only Dockers or some similarly priced knock-off brand.

"Then you thought you'd pound on the door of a business that wasn't even open yet, just so that you could volunteer to haul out some spare human body parts?"

"Okay, I can see how that sounds, but don't put words in my mouth. Arturo let me in here... *dragged* me in here... and the only 'relationship' I have to this place isn't so much with the owners as it is with Tim Snow..." Nick instantly regretted having blurted out Tim's name. There was no reason for him to be involved in this mess, but it was too late now. Where the hell was Tim, anyway? He was the only reason Nick happened to be in San Francisco this morning in the first place.

The quieter of the two policemen, the one who was writing everything down, said, "Tim, that's T – I – M, short for Timothy?"

"Yes," Nick mumbled under his breath.

"And Snow as in 'winter snow'?"

Nick spelled it out slowly, one letter at a time, but sarcasm was beyond the reach of this particular member of San Francisco's "finest."

"And what is Mr. Snow's relationship to you?"

"He's my boyfriend," Nick said. Hell, this was Castro Street, after all. The police should be used to this. "He might have been my legal husband by now if it hadn't been for Proposition 8 and the fact that he was in a wheelchair for most of last winter."

"Wheelchair? What does that have to do with...?"

"He was too vain to be in a wheelchair for the wedding pictures."

"Whatever... does this Mr. Snow have employment here?" the officer asked, frowning.

"He did before the accident," Nick said. "He was a waiter... oh good... here's Aunt Ruth. She always knows what to do. Ruth, thank God you're here!" Nick yelled out and everyone turned their attention toward the front door.

Ruth came bustling in, replaced the chair in the open doorway and put the *CLOSED* sign back where she'd found it. Then she plopped her purse on the bar and sat down on the stool next to Nick and gave him a peck on the cheek. "Nick, what on earth is going on?" Ruth wrapped one arm around his shoulder. "Arturo didn't tell me you were here too, sweetheart."

Nick had never been so happy to see her. "I *was* looking for Tim—" Nick started to answer, but he was cut off.

"I'll be the one asking the questions here, if you don't mind, Ma-am," said the burly cop.

"How do you do, officer," Ruth said, extending her hand and leaning forward. "My name is Ruth Taylor, and you are... let me see... Officer O'Sullivan, I can see that now by the inscription on your little brass badge. I am so sorry to interrupt."

"Captain O'Sullivan," he corrected. "Homicide. And this is Officer Parker, my assistant." In spite of his gruff exterior, the policeman was visibly affected by the presence of a lady. The tension in his jaw and shoulders relaxed a little and his voice softened. "Now then... where were we? Oh, yes... you said that Mr. Snow was in an accident. Do you mean those were his hands lodged in the sewage pipes?"

"Accident!" Ruth cried out. "I just left Tim beside the pool at Sam's in Hillsborough and he was fine. Who got their hands stuck in a pipe? Where's Arturo?"

"Then you do know Arturo, Miss Taylor?" Captain O'Sullivan asked. "Perhaps you can help us. You are Mr. Musgrove's Aunt, I take it?"

"No, sir," Ruth corrected him. "Tim Snow is my nephew. Arturo and his partner, Artie, are my landlords around the corner on Collingwood Street. I also work for them from time to time, which is why I am here today. I understand Artie threw his back out."

"Hiya, Ruth! Welcome back," came from the direction of the front door. It was Jake, another waiter, arriving for work, followed by Scott, the redheaded bartender, and bringing up the rear was James, the other waiter. "Cheese it, it's the fuzz!" Jake said in a loud stage whisper. James started laughing and held his wrists together as if he were turning himself in to be handcuffed.

Captain O'Sullivan was not amused. "The *CLOSED* sign at the door seems to do little good," he said to no one in particular. "Maybe we'd better lock it for the time being."

"That's okay, Officer," Ruth said. "They all work here."

"And Arturo wanted to air the place out. It doesn't smell so bad anymore, does it guys?" Nick asked the new arrivals.

"No worse than usual," Jake said.

"I'll need sworn statements from each of you," Captain O'Sullivan said. "Were you all working here last night?"

"Yes," James answered. "All except for Nick and Ruth. Nick doesn't work here. How's it going, Nick? Are you working brunch today, Ruth?"

"Please give Officer Parker your names, phone numbers and a current address where you can be reached. I also need the names of any other employees and to the best of your recollection any customers who might have used the ladies' restroom last night."

"Customers!" Jake said. "There were dozens of customers. It was Saturday night! Since this is the Castro, there maybe weren't as many women as men, but that doesn't rule out anyone using the ladies' room. I've used it myself when there was a line at the men's and no one else in there."

Ruth stood up and went behind the bar, started opening refrigerators and pulling out mixers, juice and bar fruit. Scott filled a bucket from the ice machine and carried it behind the bar. He said, "I suppose you could get some idea of who was in for dinner last night from the reservation book."

"It's right here on the corner of the bar," Ruth slid it over to Officer Parker, since he was doing all the writing.

"There were lots of walk-ins, though," James said. "Just when we thought it was quieting down, we got a party of 10 around 9:30. I took them and then Jake got a few late deuces right afterward."

"Phil had a big crowd around the piano, too," Jake said. "A lot of them didn't eat. They just came in for drinks, but any one of them could have used the ladies' room. There was that old queen who used to be on Broadway... in the chorus, no doubt. He hadn't been in since his stroke. He gets drunk and tells stories about working with Carol Channing and what a foul mouth Julie Andrews had. You wouldn't think it, would you? She was Mary Poppins and she played a nun."

"Don't forget; she was topless in *10*," James said.

Scott corrected him, "No, it was *S.O.B.*"

"That's right, I forgot. Well, anyway, when you get a few drinks in that guy he's kind of loud, but he sure can belt out the old show tunes."

Captain O'Sullivan shook his head as Officer Parker tried to write everything down. "Does Carol Channing spell her name with an 'e' on the end of Carol or not?" he asked Jake.

"I don't think so," Jake said.

"Never mind that," yelled Captain O'Sullivan.

"You could probably get some more names of who was here last night by looking at the credit card receipts," Ruth said, trying to be helpful.

"Friday was the 15th of the month, though," James said. "A lot of people get paid on the 1st and the 15th, so there was more cash than usual. Still, there were some charges. You could ask Artie. He keeps track of them behind the bar and then he figures out our tips that are on the charge slips at the end of the night. Where is Artie, anyway?"

"He threw his back out," Ruth said.

"I was afraid of that," Scott said. "I told him not to try to lift that keg by himself, but he's been on such a health kick lately, losing weight and exercising. He suddenly thinks he's a he-man or something."

"We'll need to question this Artie person, of course," said Officer Parker, scratching his head with his pen. "I also heard someone mention an employee named Phil, I believe?"

"Phil is the piano player. He'll be in a little later," Scott explained. "He doesn't have to do a lot of set-up before work like the rest of us."

Jake and James were putting out silverware, napkins and coffee cups on all the tables. "Unless you count filing his nails," Jake said. "I think he keeps his manicure in good shape for his other job, though."

"He's a high-class hooker, that's for sure," James added.

"We'll definitely need to interview him, as well," said Officer Parker.

"But, Sergeant O'Brien..." Ruth pleaded.

"Captain O'Sullivan," he corrected her.

"I beg your pardon," she said. "I am so sorry, but you have me terribly flustered, sir, and your arm was covering your name tag when you leaned against the bar like that... Captain O'Sullivan..."

"It's quite alright, ma-am."

"I wasn't even in the city last night, but I've been working with most of these nice young men off and on for months now, since shortly after I arrived in San Francisco, as a matter of fact. I can vouch for the character and integrity of each and every one of them without hesitation. I have also known Nick for almost as long, even though he doesn't work here. He doesn't even live here in the city, in fact."

"Get his address," O'Sullivan barked.

"Here's my business card," Nick replied.

"But, Captain," Ruth went on. "You seem intent on questioning everyone here as if we were suspects in some kind of crime. All I know is that the plumbing got plugged up, Artie's back went out over a beer keg, someone got their hand stuck in a pipe and what else did Arturo tell me…?"

"The dumpster," Nick added, grimly.

"Yes, I think he might have mentioned the dumpster too," Ruth repeated. "Thank you, Nick. I rarely have any reason to visit the dumpster myself, but can you please tell us what's going on here? If one of us is being accused of having stolen something, I'm sure we'd all like to know."

"Something was lost, Ruth, not stolen," Nick said. "Arturo and I found some fingers…"

"Fingers?" Ruth asked as she poured a fresh pot of water into the coffee maker. "I thought you said they were stuck."

"Ahem!" Captain O'Sullivan shook his head and waited until Ruth turned around again to face him. When the room was silent and he had everyone's undivided attention, he said, "Someone has apparently lost their hands and Mr. Musgrove here seems to have discovered them in the dumpster while cleaning up the debris that clogged the sewer pipes."

"Don't forget the eyeball," Officer Parker said.

"Oh, yes," Captain O'Sullivan said. "Parts of two hands have been found that were clogging up the pipes… *and* one eyeball… so far."

# Chapter 7

"Do you want me to do you now?" Tim asked.

Adam raised his head from where he was sprawled on the deck chair and turned toward Tim. "What'd you say?"

"Do you want me to put some oil on you? That's what I meant to say..." Tim laughed. He felt tongue-tied in the presence of someone so physically perfect. He knew his face must be turning red and it had nothing to do with the sun. "I've heard that black people can get sunburned too, if they're not careful... or do you prefer African-American?"

Adam let out a long yawn. "I don't care... sure, you could rub some on my back, I suppose. What a perfect day, huh? The sun feels so good, but a person shouldn't overdo it. The vitamin D is healthy, but you don't want to dry out the skin. It ages you, you know." Adam reached into his bag and handed Tim a tube of some brand of cream he had never heard of before.

"How long will you be here in Hillsborough?" Tim unscrewed the cap and knelt beside Adam. He began to smear the odorless lotion between his broad shoulder blades and watched it dissolve into his smooth skin. Tim didn't dare straddle Adam's legs, as Adam had straddled him earlier. For one thing, Tim wasn't quite tall enough, and he was nervous already.

"I have two weeks until my next job, a magazine shoot for *Details* in L.A. I was thinking about renting a car next week and driving down the coast."

Tim was thinking about the last time he'd had sex with a black man, a stunning guy named Mario. Adam's skin was so smooth over the taut muscles of his back and shoulders that Tim couldn't help thinking about it. He'd never had a "thing" for black men... or blonds or Italians or redheads or anyone else. He considered himself lucky that he wasn't restricted in his attractions to any particular type of guy. Life held so many more options that way.

"'Just my type' means he's genetically male and breathing!" That's what Tim's co-worker Jake had said often enough and Tim felt pretty much the same way. The color of Adam's flesh reminded him of Mario. He was the only black man Tim could remember now, in fact. It was so long ago Tim wasn't sure anymore if Mario was the guy's name. He remembered the color of his skin and how he'd told Tim he was named for his Italian grandfather, but the rest of the family was Jamaican. Tim still had a snapshot of the two of them in front of Half Dome on his refrigerator at home. They'd driven to Yosemite one fine spring day when Tim still had his old black Mustang.

"How about you?" Adam asked. Tim tensed a little, remembering where he was, and then he squeezed more lotion out of the tube.

"Huh?"

"How long are you staying here in Hillsborough?"

"Oh... not long... I just stopped by to say good-bye to my Aunt Ruth. I'm driving down to L.A. Hey, maybe you could ride along with me." Tim knew he was stretching the truth a little. He'd planned to head down the coast, but he hadn't made up his mind whether or not he would drive all the way to L.A.

"That's good, thanks," Adam said.

Tim realized he was still massaging Adam's back, so he stopped, put the cap on the tube and moved back to his own chair. "You're welcome... no problem."

"How soon are you heading out?"

"Um... I don't know... I didn't plan to spend the night here last night. I was only gonna let my Aunt Ruth know I was going away so she wouldn't worry." Tim stared at Adam's long muscular back and watched the sunlight play across the colors of his bare flesh. "I haven't seen her in a while. She's been spending a lot of time down here with Sam lately."

"Yes, I gathered as much. Do you have friends in L.A.?"

Tim was lost in thought, remembering Mario... or was it Marcello? Now he began to forget about Mario or Marcello or whatever his name was and think back to his last trip to L.A. He was in love with Jason at the time, but Jason was still mourning Karl, who died of AIDS before Tim entered the picture. Karl had left the house on Hancock Street to Jason and after Jason's murder the house went to Tim. Then Tim met Nick and now they were taking a break from each other.

"It's kind of a long story." Tim started to take another sip of his coffee, but it was barely lukewarm now. "Jason had some friends in L.A. that I got to know a little bit when I was down there with him."

"Jason?"

"We were... sort of an item... for a while. He's dead now—murdered—but I'm sure some of his friends would want to see me, the ones who came up to San Francisco for his memorial. We had it at the restaurant—Arts, on Castro Street—where we both worked together. They said if I was ever in L.A. to be sure to look them up. I think they'd remember me."

"I see," Adam said.

Tim felt foolish, having admitted that he didn't really have any friends in L.A. They were Jason's friends, not his. He reached for the Altoids box where he stashed the joint he'd started earlier and relit it. "Wanna hit?"

Adam looked up. "Smells good, but no thanks. You go ahead. Sorry to hear about your friend."

"It was a while ago," Tim took another long toke off the joint and tried again to remember the last time he'd made it with a black guy. "I don't like to dwell on the past." But his mind raced back to Mario... Marcello... NO, it was Martino! *That* was his name.

Tim laughed at himself, forgetting Martino's name. He could just about hear Jake right now saying, "I'll bet you remember his cock!" Man, the guy was gorgeous, too! He should have been in movies, but he worked for Hewlett Packard. Tim met him one night after work back when the Pendulum was still a black bar on 18th Street, across from the Edge. Jake was seeing one of the bartenders there and invited Tim along to keep him company while he waited for his date to get off work at 2AM.

It was about 1AM when Martino walked in with a group of friends. Tim was standing at the urinal when he came up beside him. Tim remembered the toilet in the old Pendulum, the chipped white tiles that looked as if someone had tried to spray paint them blue. They gave the room a wintery look, even when the weather was warm. Tim always expected to see his breath when he exhaled in there, whenever he was as stoned as he was right now. It felt like being inside an ice cube or a space-ship where the aliens had blue lips and cold blood.

"So you're driving to L.A.?" Adam steered the subject back on track.

"I guess so. I'm not in any big hurry. You're just getting here and I'm ready to leave. It seems a shame to take off right now. I don't want to impose on Sam though, especially when Aunt Ruth isn't even here."

"I'm sure Sam doesn't mind," Adam said. "Your cousin Dianne is still here too, right? I'm sure you're no greater imposition than she is."

"So you've met my cousin?" Tim asked with a grin.

"No, like I said, I've only *heard* about her from my mother." Adam stood up and took a few steps to the end of the pool. He dived in and let the motion propel his long body to the far end. A few easy strokes brought him back. Adam raised his head at the edge of the pool in the same spot where Tim had first laid eyes on him an hour ago. "The water is perfect. You should join me."

"Oh-oh! Speak of the devil," Tim said softly to Adam before he yelled, "Good morning, Dianne!" His cousin dashed back inside the house as if she didn't hear him. Curtains moved at the window so they knew she was watching them. "I've got a great idea, Adam. I was thinking about stopping at San Gregorio on my way down the coast. Do you want to join me?"

"The nude beach? I haven't been there since I was a teenager. It sounds great Tim, but I just got here. My mother..."

"We'd only be gone a little while," Tim interrupted. "Just for a couple of hours... I promise to have you back here in plenty of time for dinner. Sam said something about barbecuing later."

"Wait right here." Adam pulled himself up out of the pool in one smooth move. He grabbed his towel and disappeared into the house. Tim had a dip in the pool and Adam was back before Tim had climbed out of the water. "Can we wait about fifteen minutes?"

"Sure... why?" Tim asked. "I hope you didn't ask my cousin Dianne to come with us."

"No way," Adam laughed. "Mom wants to pack us lunch to take along, that's all."

"Sounds great."

Tim wasn't crazy about city driving, but with the top down and the smells of freshly mowed lawns and eucalyptus he enjoyed being behind the wheel in the country, or the suburbs, at least. He also realized that as much as he wanted an adventure by himself, he also liked having this handsome man beside him. He was so sexy and so easy to talk to. They headed north on Highway 280 for several miles until Tim said, "Adam, could you find the map in the glove box for me? There's got to be a place to cut across to the coast from here."

"Not until we get past Lake San Andreas," Adam said as he started to look for the map.

"Is that named after the San Andreas Fault?"

"No, it's the other way around; the fault is named for the lake. It was a sag pond, a dip between parallel fault lines that fills with water. They dammed it up to make Crystal Springs Reservoirs, north and south. It covers several miles along here."

"Maybe we don't need a map with you along," Tim said. "You're not only handsome, but smart, too."

Tim remembered when Martino... or was it Mariano? Anyway, the hot young black guy was riding along in the passenger seat of Tim's old black Mustang on their way to Yosemite. They'd spent the night together in Tim's bed on Collingwood Street and decided to get up early and have an adventure on hardly any sleep. Mariano was handsome too. Tim remembered him going through the glove compartment looking at old music cassette tape mixes, popping them in and pulling them out again. Then he turned on the car radio and found a station Tim hated. The sex with Mariano had been great, but Tim started regretting this Yosemite idea when he realized the vast gap in their tastes in music.

"I grew up here, you know," Adam said and Tim came back to the present. Adam had found the map and refolded it to spread northern California across his knees. "It's been a while, though. I majored in Geology before I got into modeling. Hey Tim, look what else I found in the glove box. Is this the cell phone you promised your Aunt Ruth you'd keep turned on?"

"That's the one. Do you know how to work it?"

"I think I can figure it out. Where do you turn it on?"

"I don't know, somewhere on the side there. I've never really used it. I hate the damned things. Nick bought it for me for Christmas, but I've resisted learning."

"Really? I thought everyone had a cell phone these days."

"Everyone else does, maybe. Can't I be different? Everywhere you go, people are talking and texting and tweeting. I was the last person I knew to buy a computer, too. The only reason I got one of those was so I could cruise the dating sites. Do you use dude surfer?

"What?"

"Dude surfer dot com. It's a hook-up site, *my* personal favorite."

"I've never even heard of it."

"Maybe it's not that big back in Chicago. There are so many of them nowadays, aren't there? You could spend your whole life on-line. Since I met Nick I haven't nearly as much, of course." Tim knew he was still a little buzzed from that joint earlier. He was talking too much.

At Pacifica they turned south onto Highway 1 and drove into a thick bank of fog. "Damn, I wasn't counting on this," Tim said. "It was so hot in Hillsborough. This fog is as thick as it is in the city half the time."

"It's probably too cold for any nude beaches, but we could head north. It looks clearer in that direction and at least we can pull over somewhere."

"I guess so."

"What else was your Aunt Ruth was trying to get at, besides promising to turn on your cell phone?"

"Do you mean… about Nick?" Tim pulled onto a scenic overlook.

"I guess so… white meat or dark?" Adam reached for the picnic basket behind the seats.

"Nick is white… *blond*, even… oh, you mean the chicken. I'll take a breast."

"Yeah, that was it." Adam handed Tim a piece of fried chicken in a paper towel. "Who's Nick? You mentioned him earlier, too."

"He's my boyfriend. He's really wonderful, but…" Tim started to take a bite. "Wow… this chicken is delicious."

"But what? It seemed like something important, at least to your aunt."

"He is," Tim said. "Nick is very important to me. It's just that I was laid up all winter and he had to take care of me. I think he must be really sick of looking at me like that, feeding me, washing me, emptying bedpans... you know."

"He must really love you."

"I guess so... maybe I'm just being silly, trying to give us a break from each other. Have you ever had anyone like that in your life?"

"I do now," Adam said. "Alex is like that for me. Did you stick that issue of *Vanity Fair* in your bag? Look at page 97."

"Another model?" asked Tim, reaching for his backpack.

"Yeah, we met on a job in Atlanta last summer—the most beautiful person I've ever known—inside and out."

"Let's see..." Tim wiped his hands on a napkin and flipped through the magazine. "Page ninety-seven? That's a lipstick ad. I thought you said Alex. There's a girl on that page."

"Isn't she beautiful? That's my Alexandra. We're getting married around Christmas."

# Chapter 8

Life at Sam's Hillsborough estate moved at a snail's pace compared to the hustle and bustle of Castro Street. No sooner had the police left Arts than the crowds poured in. A customer at one of Jake's first tables ordered a dry Rob Roy and Ruth had to stop and think how to make one. *Hmmm... a regular Rob Roy is scotch and sweet vermouth with a cherry, so a dry Rob Roy must use dry vermouth instead. And probably a lemon twist for garnish.* "Jake, who's ordering Rob Roy's at brunch? That's a dinnertime drink. Did you tell them what good Bloody Marys we make here? Push the Bloody Marys. Tell them they're on special."

"It's for that lady in the green hat with the two really cute guys in leather. She must be the mother of one of them."

Ruth reached for the *Old Mr. Boston Bartender's Guide* that Artie kept in the drawer between the cash registers. She fingered through the tattered pages until she found the recipe. "If it's for somebody's mother I'd better make it good," she muttered. "My feet hurt already and it's going to be a long day."

If only she'd taken the time to stop at Collingwood and change into more comfortable shoes. All she would have missed was a few extra minutes of the police asking her questions she couldn't answer. But Arturo had been so insistent on the phone that they needed her help, and Ruth loved to feel needed more than she hated to admit she was growing older. If Artie could still work as hard as he did, she ought to be able to as well.

News of the findings in the dumpster spread fast. Ruth suspected most of the gossip flying around was wrong. Despite the rumors, no weapon had been found. No arrest had been made. And she actually overheard a couple of men suggesting that diamond rings covered the severed fingers as if they belonged to Liberace!

A pair of police cars, still parked nose-to-nose in front of the restaurant, blocked one lane of traffic on Castro Street and drew even more attention to the place. Ruth thought the grisly news of body parts in the restaurant's plumbing might have kept people away, but not on Castro Street. The telephone and the Internet had spread the word too and stirred up a lot of folks' curiosity. Someone insisted that a Rolex watch was still ticking inside a latex glove on a severed arm. Ruth shook her head. How did so much misinformation get started?

After the policemen left, Nick stayed for an omelet, toast and coffee, as well as to give Ruth some sane company for the first hour. He was the only one at the bar who wasn't involved in some kind of wild speculation. She served him a Bloody Mary that he didn't order. "What's this?" he asked.

"It's a mistake," Ruth whispered. She'd learned that old trick from Artie, who used it whenever he wanted someone to stick around. "I made one too many for that table in the corner, so it's on the house. Besides, you look like you could use a drink."

"Thanks, Ruth." Nick lifted the glass and took a sip. "Tasty mistake." He smacked his lips in appreciation. "But I'd better not have more than one."

"Are you going back to the Russian River already?"

He shrugged. "I don't know what I should do. The police said they want to talk to me again, but that I could go home for now. I only came into town to see Tim. I have contractors coming to the nursery again tomorrow morning. I might drive over to Alameda and say hello to my mom and dad and visit with them and my grandmother this afternoon. I could wait and drive back to Monte Rio tonight.

"I'm sure your family would love to see you. And please give my regards to Amanda." Ruth already knew Nick's paternal grandmother, Amanda Musgrove, the mystery writer. The two women had hit it off from the start when they met here at Arts before Christmas last year.

"Did Tim tell you how long he plans to stay in Hillsborough?" Nick asked. "Did he say when he was coming back home?"

"No, he didn't say, but I can't imagine he'll stay there long. He mentioned something about taking a drive along the coast, but it's awfully foggy for that today. I'm sure Sam would like Tim to stay and visit longer, but everything's up in the air since I had to rush back to work this morning. And my daughter Dianne is there, too. That's a whole other story in itself..."

Ruth thought back to the last time Nick came to town unexpectedly, the night he discovered Tim in the Midnight Sun with a drunken, but very sexy, young athlete from the UCLA track team. He was someone's nephew, either Theodore or Leonardo's. Ruth couldn't remember anymore and it didn't matter. She just knew how hurt Nick had been over a misunderstanding. Now she couldn't get the image of Delia's handsome son Adam out of her mind. She pictured those long, dark fingers rubbing suntan oil into the small of her nephew's back and her mind's eye zoomed in on them sliding along the elastic waist band of Tim's shorts. She wanted to erase the image, as if Nick could read her mind. "You should give Tim a call."

"Don't you think I've tried? All I get is that old answering machine of his when I call him at home and he never picks up his new cell phone I bought him for Christmas."

"I'll bet he would now. I told him just before I left to keep it handy so I can reach him on it. You should try calling him again."

"I don't know." Nick finished off the drink, then sucked on an ice cube a moment. "He said he needed a break or he thought I needed a break. Sometimes I just don't understand what's going on in his mind."

"You know what? Back in Minnesota people talk about something called 'cabin fever.' I think Tim might have a touch of that. It comes from being snowed in during the winter with that sense that you just want to break out and go someplace... anyplace. I'll bet Tim felt a bit of cabin fever being cooped up after the accident. He must have made a terrible patient."

"Tell me about it," Nick agreed with a chuckle.

"Try him on the cell phone again, dear."

When the brunch rush finally wound down, Ruth wondered why she was even here. It would have been so much nicer to stay in Hillsborough with Sam and Tim, to have gone ahead with the barbecue, even with Dianne under foot and so unpredictable. It would feel good to have Sam put his arms around her right now. He was always such a comfort. She looked up from washing glasses and was shocked to see a very pale-looking Artie coming in the front door.

"What are you doing out of bed?" Scott asked. "I didn't think we'd see you again for at least a week."

Artie sat down on a bar stool at the center of the bar where he could talk to both bartenders at once. "I just crawled out of my death bed to see how you two were getting along without me," he said. "Fix me a mild Bloody Mary, one of you... please? It will go great with my Vicodin and muscle relaxers."

"Are you sure it's okay to mix, Artie?" Ruth asked.

"I'm not driving."

"That's not what I mean and you know it."

"The worse thing that can happen is that I'll gain weight. How many calories are in a Bloody Mary, anyway? I'm trying to take off at least another ten pounds so I can fit into my old gowns. Mark my words, one of these days I'm gonna surprise everyone. I'm gonna work my old act back into shape and Artie Glamóur will make the biggest come-back since—"

"In the meantime..." Scott interrupted. "What about tonight? You're not planning to come back to work behind the bar, are you?"

Artie reached for the reservation book and flipped it open to see how busy the evening was shaping up to be. "I hate to ask, but could either of you darlings pull a double?"

"Yes, Artie," they both answered at once, and Ruth added, "I just have to go home and get some different shoes. These are killing my feet."

Scott said, "And Artie... you have to promise not to try juggling any more beer kegs by yourself in the future. Next time you need a keg changed, if I'm not close by, get one of the waiters or a busboy to help you."

"I know. I know. If I really wanted the exercise I'd go join the gym like you young fellas do. Can't you just see me tossing those weights around, lifting dumbbells and cowbells?"

"I think you mean barbells, Artie," Scott said with a grin.

"Not to change the subject, but Arturo called me at home and told me about the police interrogations this morning. I'm sorry everybody had to go through all that. Were they horrid to you?"

"Well, they didn't send any gay cops this time; let's put it that way," Scott said. "You'll get your turn to be subjected to their questions. They wanted to come and yank you out of bed when they left here this morning, but Arturo convinced them you were so drugged up you were practically in a coma."

"God bless him."

"They'll want to speak to you as soon as they can, though," Ruth said. "They wanted to know if there were any other employees too, and I wasn't sure. I told them I only work part time. They talked to Scott and me and Arturo, of course, plus James and Jake and Phil, when he came in a little later. Who else is there, Artie?"

"Well, there's Tim, of course, but he hasn't been around much since the accident. Let me think... there's Pablo, the new busboy. He just started this week—he's another one of Arturo's nephews—but they'll need a translator to get anything out of him. He *was* working last night, though."

"I haven't met him yet, then. Does he know about Jorge, the boy who was murdered last year? They're not related, are they?"

"Who knows? They could be cousins. I leave Arturo in charge of the kitchen help. I imagine Pablo must have heard the history about this place, about Jorge and Jason and the others, but at least *we* know *that* killer is dead."

Ruth cringed at the memory of putting the fireplace poker through the killer cowboy's back. "Thank heaven!"

"Is there anyone else, Artie?" Scott asked.

"There's Danny, the accountant, but he's only here in the morning about once or twice a month, usually on Tuesdays. Then there's that adorable boy who delivers our flower arrangement every week from Ixia, but he comes on Thursday afternoons and I wouldn't exactly call him an employee. He did come to the Christmas party last year, though. Did you see his hunky boyfriend? Oh, the stuff that dreams are made of—wet dreams, I mean."

"What about Patrick?" Ruth remembered Patrick, the waiter. He worked there before she arrived in San Francisco. He reminded her of dozens of good-looking young Minnesota boys–blond and blue-eyed Scandinavians. "Whatever became of him? He was the one who was dealing drugs, right?" Ruth was proud of what she considered the sophistication of her question. When she'd first heard Arturo and Artie say that Patrick was dealing, she assumed they meant cards.

"Yes. Patrick," Artie sighed. "He did come back when he got out of the Betty Ford Clinic, but he only worked a few shifts. It was right after Tim's accident and we'd already hired James. We didn't need Patrick during the winter months when business was slower. Now that the tourists are starting to trickle back in, I wouldn't mind giving him a shift here and there, but I was hoping Tim would be back by then."

"I'm sure Tim will be eager to get back to work when he's a little stronger, Artie," Ruth said.

Jake was ordering drinks from Scott at the waiters' station when he overheard his former co-worker's name. "Hi, Artie. How's your back? What were y'all saying about Patrick?"

"My back is somewhat better. I'm feeling no pain at the moment, thanks to Vicodin and one of Ruth's marvelous Bloody Marys. Jake, have you seen Patrick lately?"

"Yeah I have, come to think of it. I usually stop by Moby's when I get out of here on Saturday nights if I can make it in time for last call. I run into Patrick quite a lot. I didn't see him last night, though."

"You've seen him drinking?" Artie set his Bloody Mary down on the bar for a moment. "Don't they tell you not to drink when you're trying to stay off drugs? I hope he doesn't go back on that nasty stuff."

"The policemen also wanted to know who has access to the dumpster," Ruth said. "We assumed that the severed fingers were all that was plugging up the pipes, but the police didn't have any proof of that."

"The plumbing has so many twists and turns, anyway," Artie said. "If they were plugging things up, they could have come from anywhere on the block. They didn't necessarily go down the toilet from our little girls' room. But, you were asking about access to the dumpsters?"

"The police were," Ruth said. "I just wanted to warn you what to expect when they question you."

"They'll want to talk to Al… Al Marino. He owns the card shop next-door and they use our dumpster… oh, and there's Al's brother Ed. He just bought the apartment building directly behind us. The only access to the back for the garbage men is through their driveway. They have their own dumpster on the other side, but if ours is full we use theirs and vice versa. The lock on that gate from the Hartford Street alley has been broken for years. And even if it was locked, that fence is so low that anyone could jump over it."

"I didn't know there was access to Hartford Street through the back," Ruth said.

"That's because we've never asked you to haul out the garbage," Artie said. "The video store has access, too. We pay the monthly garbage bill for all three of us, since we have the most trash. Al writes us a nominal check every three months that we apply to our quarterly taxes. The lesbians at the video store use our dumpster and give us free rentals in exchange. They hardly have any trash, really—maybe a wastebasket full of paper each day and some cardboard when they get shipments of new DVDs. Most of that goes in the recycling bin."

"That makes sense," Ruth wiped down the bar in front of Artie and replaced his dampened cocktail napkin.

"Thanks. I spilled a little. Do you want me to put your name on the free movie list, Ruth? It's no problem."

"Hey, I just pre-paid them forty bucks for twenty rentals," Scott said.

"I'm sorry, Scott. I should have told you," said Artie. "Of course, you'd probably abuse the privilege with pornography and ruin it for all of us."

"I beg your pardon! You must be thinking of Jake or Phil… or Tim!" But Tim wasn't there and Jake and Phil were too far away to hear him.

"There was something else about the dumpster, though – something important," Ruth said. "I know! They asked who'd been painting. They found a bunch of paint cans in there. I told them I didn't recall you painting anything in here."

"No, we haven't painted anything lately. The last thing Arturo painted was that wall behind the piano, but that was months ago. I think Viv was still playing here then. Yes, I remember she said the color clashed with her skin tones."

Ruth thought back to "Vivacious Vivian," the piano player who was working at Arts when she first came out to visit Tim. Ruth never cared much for the woman, but she felt a little sorry for her. Ruth hadn't meant to kill Viv's husband, but it was either his life or Tim's. "I wonder how Viv is doing these days."

"She sent a postcard from Paris a few weeks ago. Didn't you see it? Arturo stuck it up on the bulletin board outside the bathrooms, but it must have fallen off. Anyway… speaking of paint cans… you can't just put them in a dumpster. You have to dispose of them properly."

Jake stood at the waiters' station listening, but he didn't have a drink order. "It's probably even more illegal to dump body parts than paint cans, Artie." The brunch rush was either at a lull or the busiest part of the day was over. Jake started folding linen napkins for the dinner shift.

All the policemen's comments and questions were roiling through the back of Ruth's mind. She was sure everything would straighten itself out if she just gave it a rest. Right now she needed to go back to Collingwood and change her shoes. How she wished she had time to give her feet a long soak, but it would soon be time to get ready for the dinner crowd. Somehow she and Scott had let themselves get talked into working a double, even though she'd much rather be in Hillsborough with Sam right now.

# Chapter 9

Tim dropped the *Vanity Fair* magazine. It closed in his lap and slipped through his legs to the floor of the Thunderbird. Now he wished he could crawl down there under the floor mat. He couldn't remember when he'd felt so foolish.

"You thought I was gay, huh?" Adam said. "I get that all the time."

"Why didn't you stop me? You let me carry on like a blithering idiot." Tim picked up the magazine and took another look at the advertisement with Adam's fiancée, Alexandra, before he tossed it into the back seat. "She really is beautiful. I'm sure you'll make a lovely couple and have adorable children."

"Come on, Tim... I'm sorry, okay? I have lots of gay friends. It's no big deal. I hope you and I can be friends, too. You're a great guy."

It was one thing to be passed over for another *man*. Tim thought of all the hours he'd spent checking out a stranger in a bar. It could be his Roman nose or the way his pants fit. Tim might have liked the shape of his face or fallen for something that was only temporary, like his sideburns or his radical haircut or his T-shirt with a funny slogan on the front. He just *knew* the stranger's smile was meant for him.

Then Tim would buy a fresh drink because "Mr. Wonderful" had just bought another beer. And Tim would be thinking how fateful it was that he had a cold six-pack of the same brand in the fridge at home and how he'd put clean sheets on the bed that afternoon. It must be an omen. He'd take a deep breath and start toward him, sure that the stars were all aligned in his favor and that he never looked better in his life. Then three steps away from the man of his dreams there'd be a tap on his shoulder, "Excuse me."

And that was when Tim realized that the handsome stranger's smile was meant for the man behind him, now trying to get by. At least it was another *guy*.

"I was even thinking about showing you off at the beach!

"Huh?"

"Aw, this'll sound crazy, but the last time I was at San Gregorio, I was with Jason and..." Tim's voice trailed off. Whenever Tim went anywhere with Jason it felt like they were showing off. It was mostly because everyone *knew* Jason, but it was partly that Tim looked good, too. The two of them looked good together, better than either of them looked individually and when other guys eyed them with envy, Tim was secretly very happy.

"Now, which one was Jason again?"

"My ex... but he's dead... the murdered one."

"Oh yeah, sorry."

"There's just something about two hot guys together." Tim felt tongue-tied in his embarrassment. "Now that I know you're not gay, it's hard to explain. And I know I'm nowhere near as hot as you, but when the energy is right between two guys, when they're really into each other, they give off sort of an aura. I guess I miss that with Jason and I was fantasizing about how great you would look at the nude beach, like if... if it weren't such a cloudy day and if... if all sorts of people I knew happened to be there. They'd all be so jealous! I know it's silly. I must sound shallow and stupid and now I'm stoned on top of it."

"Don't you and Nick have that... that *aura* when you two are together?"

"Nick and I *should*. It's just that we're hardly ever out together out in public. Or I'm at work when he comes into the restaurant and then we go straight home. Or when I'm up at the river I'm usually with him at his place. It used to be with Jason that everywhere we went I felt like people were looking at us to see who he was with and it made me kind of happy, like I was the one who had snagged the biggest prize."

"Uh-huh," Adam tried to be polite by letting Tim continue.

"I suppose Nick and I might turn a few heads at the Rainbow in the off-season, but that's a far cry from being naked at San Gregorio. Don't you feel that way with Alex when the two of you go someplace together?"

"I guess so."

"I'm sorry. I must sound like a real jerk. This just proves you can't make assumptions about people, huh? I'm so embarrassed."

"Hey, I'm flattered, really. Don't sweat it. In my business, it happens a lot. Most of the guys I work with are gay, probably more of the photographers and designers than the models, but we all get along well enough to get the job done. I know a lot of people whose sexual preference is the mirror. That doesn't make them gay, just narcissistic."

Tim tried to laugh, but he could only nod in agreement.

"Besides, you make 'straight' sound like a dirty word or some awful disease... or worse, like 'square' or 'boring.' I don't think anyone is totally anything. You must have heard of the Kinsey Scale."

"What?"

"Alfred Kinsey. A  sex researcher back in the 50s or 60s. They made a movie out of his life with Liam Neeson and Laura Linney. It was pretty good.

Tim nodded, remembering. "Nick rented that one night when I was laid up. I must have fallen asleep through it. Again."

"Kinsey developed this scale where if a person was totally heterosexual he was a zero and someone who was totally homosexual was a six."

"That must be where the Kinsey Sicks got their name."

"You lost me."

"They're an a cappella drag group that started out in San Francisco. They sing, but they're also really funny. They perform all over the world now." When Tim saw the lost look on Adam's face, he grinned. "Sorry, I didn't mean to change the subject. But I got their holiday CD for a present. It's called *Oy Vey in a Manger*." Tim laughed.

"So most people fall somewhere in between on the Kinsey Scale, if they're honest about it." Adam grabbed another piece of his mother's fried chicken and popped the top off a beer. "Do you want a beer?" he offered the can to Tim.

"Maybe later. I'd better take you back to Hillsborough and then be on my way."

"What's the rush?" Adam asked. "It's starting to clear. We could still go to the beach if you want. Let's drive south a ways and check it out."

Tim started the ignition, then headed down Highway 1 but he knew he wouldn't go to the beach now. What was he thinking, as pale as he was? The closest he'd been to being naked all winter was when Nick bathed him, but there was always a cast here, a bandage there. Now the sun was shining through the salty ocean air and one of the most beautiful men Tim had ever seen was in the passenger's seat of the Thunderbird with the top down and the guy was straight.

"Well, it *is* turning into a nice day," Adam said as they drove south along the coast, "but I think it's still too cold for the beach."

"That's okay. I don't feel like climbing all those stairs anyway." Tim tried to collect his thoughts, even though he was still flustered with embarrassment. "You know, the last time I was here we saw a whale just off-shore. It splashed and spouted back and forth all afternoon. Hundreds of people were lined up from one end of the beach to the other. They cheered like it was a circus act. The whale seemed to know it was putting on a show for all those naked fans."

"Maybe it was. Whales are pretty smart."

"Sure... I guess... maybe it was. So... where do you fall on the Kinsey Scale, Adam? Don't tell me you're one of those *down-low* brothers, cheating on their wives and girlfriends with gay guys and bringing home cooties... or worse!"

Adam laughed. "No, I'm totally turned on by Alexandra. Wait til you meet her, she's gorgeous. I still don't want to be thought of as a square, though. I suppose I'd have to say I'm a one on the Kinsey Scale. I don't have any plans to cheat on my wife when we're married, but I don't think anyone is a zero or a six."

"I am. Definitely a six!" Tim insisted. But it got him thinking. He'd always liked women. Aside from his mother, he'd had mostly good relationships with women. There were lots of women he could honestly say that he loved, like his Aunt Ruth, of course. There was his friend Jill from high school. Tim wondered what she was doing these days. Maybe he could track her down on Facebook or something. And he loved Sarah, the magic child. She was just a little girl now, but someday she would grow up to be a woman and Tim knew he would always love her. And he loved Jane, Sarah's mother, Tim's downstairs neighbor and tenant. He just didn't love any of them *that way.*

They were quiet for a while, admiring the views as they drove south along the cliffs and then Adam said, "I hope you're not mad at me, Tim. I probably should have told you earlier, but I wasn't sure when—"

"The best time would have been the minute you first stuck your head out of the swimming pool back in Hillsborough," Tim said. "But it must be hard to go through life introducing yourself with: 'Hello, I'm Adam. I happen to be gorgeous, but I'm straight.'"

Then a mischievous thought struck him. If Adam was a one on the Kinsey Scale, did that mean he was do-able? He'd just said he didn't plan to cheat on his wife *when they were married.* He didn't say anything about *before.* Tim glanced over at those brown muscled calves sticking out of a pair of khaki cargo shorts. Adam's long elegant fingers tapped on the dashboard in time to the music from the car radio – "Bad Romance" by Lady Gaga. Hmmm, Adam was the one who'd been fiddling with the dial and landed on this station. Were straight guys into Lady Gaga?

"Another part of me was also flattered, I have to admit," Adam said. "Gay men are known for having the best taste. Friends?"

"Friends… maybe you'll even come and visit me in San Francisco sometime. I could show you off in the Castro."

"Deal!" Adam laughed and extended his hand for a very butch hand shake.

As sexy as Adam was, Tim didn't think he could go there. He thought of his co-worker Jake and his on-going monthly trysts with his straight married dentist in the back room of the Mission News book store. Nah… Tim could never do that.

Then he thought back to a long-ago time in Minneapolis when he was a little boy at the babysitter's house around the corner. He found a piece of hard candy on the floor under the couch and picked it up and held it to the light. Tim could still picture it now. He could almost taste it, red and shiny with only a tiny piece of lint that he brushed off easily. The babysitter smacked it out of his hand, picked it up from where it landed and carried it to the kitchen trash can. Tim laughed at the thought of having sex with Adam or any other straight guy when he remembered what the babysitter had said: "Don't put that in your mouth; you don't know where it's been!"

Nah, Tim didn't need to mess around with straight guys. He had Nick. If only Nick wasn't so tired of him.

"What are you laughing at?" Adam asked.

"Nothing. I was just thinking about Jake… one of the guys at work. I'll probably have to go back to work soon, at least part time. I'm a waiter at this restaurant called Arts where my Aunt Ruth tends bar sometimes. Arturo is the chef and his lover, Artie, is an old—I should say 'former,' not 'old'—drag queen from Finocchios."

"In North Beach? Wasn't that place famous years ago?"

"That's the place. They tell me Artie was a headliner there. A lot of drag queens just lip sync, but Artie can really sing."

"Like Ru Paul or like that Kinsey group?"

"Hmmm... More like Donna Sachet, but Artie is lots older. Donna Sachet sings live too and she's local, so far, but she has a huge following. She'll be famous everywhere soon. That's the trouble. These great performers get started in San Francisco and then it just can't hold them."

"Sure, that happened a lot in North Beach. There's this little club called the Hungry i where Bill Cosby used to perform... and Mort Sahl and Barbra Streisand."

"Really? Streisand? Artie keeps talking about getting his act together again, but I guess he's gained a lot of weight since the old days at Finocchios."

"I remember hearing about that place years ago when I was just a kid. I think it was just up the street from the Hungry i."

"That's right. I forget you grew up around here. Finocchios was already closed by the time I moved out to California from Minnesota. Anyway, if you come to San Francisco you could see Arts and I could introduce you around. I don't know why you'd be interested, though..."

"Why not?"

"And I could show you the house I inherited on Hancock Street. It's a duplex. I live in the upstairs flat and Jane and Ben live downstairs with their two little kids, Sarah and Samuel Timothy. He's named after Sam and me. Come to think of it, maybe you know them... Jane is Sam's daughter. Jane must have lived at Sam's place during some of the years when you were growing up there. And they must have come to visit him since then. Maybe you were around at the same time?"

"Ben and Jane Larson," Adam said.

"Yeah. And Sarah, Sam's granddaughter. She's such a bright little girl. I call her 'the magic child' because there's something so special about her. She calls me 'Uncle Tim' and she calls Nick 'Uncle Nick.' I've never wanted kids of my own, but it's great having them nearby and getting to watch them grow up."

"I'd like to have ten," Adam said. "Alex said she'll have two and if we want any more we can adopt. She doesn't want any right away, though. Her career is hot right now. She doesn't want to take the time off and she's worried about her figure."

"Maybe you should adopt the first eight and then have two when she's ready to retire from modeling," Tim suggested.

"I'll suggest that to her," Adam said, laughing. "Do you and Nick ever think about raising children?"

"We're too old. I'm over 30 now and Nick is nearly 40."

"That's not old!"

"So... if you know Ben and Jane, you must have met the magic child too, huh?"

"Sarah?" Adam asked. "Yes, I know her. I haven't seen her new brother yet, though, but I hope to soon. I've been in Europe for a while. She calls me 'Uncle Adam' too. She's part of the reason I'd like to have kids. I'm sure when Alex meets her, she'll feel the same way."

"I guess she calls everyone 'Uncle,'" Tim said. "Well, not my Aunt Ruth, of course. She calls her 'Aunt Ruth,' naturally. Listen to me. I've been talking a mile a minute today. Anyway, I hope you'll come and see me sometime. You could meet Nick and see the kids. It's cute that Sarah calls you 'Uncle Adam.'"

"Well..." Adam paused. "There's no reason she shouldn't call me her uncle. I *am* her uncle."

"I feel the same way."

"No, you don't understand. Sarah is my niece. Jane is my half-sister. We have the same father—Sam Connor."

"Oh, my God..." Tim didn't know which was more the surprise... the news that Adam was Sam's son or that Adam was straight.. "Does my Aunt Ruth know?"

"My father said he'd tell her before he proposes, but he wanted us to get to know each other first—Ruth and me, I mean—not you and me, although it's kind of funny how that worked out. Before today I'd only met her once, at the airport in Paris last winter. It was too bad she had to drive back into the city this morning, before we had the chance to spend any more time together. With her daughter there too, it added another element that my father wasn't counting on."

*The 1812 Overture* started playing as Adam talked. Tim thought at first that it was only his imagination, but the music grew louder. "Do you hear that?"

"I think it's your cell phone. You stuck it in your bag, remember?"

"Oh, I've never heard it do that before. Will you grab it for me?" Tim slowed the car and pulled over to the side of the road where they looked out over miles of the blue Pacific and Adam handed him the phone. "Hello! This is Tim. Hello? Oh, Hiya, Aunt Ruth! Boy, have I got some news for you!"

Adam put his index finger to his mouth and shook his head. Tim caught his gesture and nodded, giving him an OKAY sign with his thumb and forefinger.

"We're out for a drive, me and Adam. No, I haven't heard from Nick yet. Have you? Why? Okay, I'll tell you my big news first. Adam is straight! Yeah, who would have guessed, huh? Now, it's your turn."

Tim listened for some time, all the while nodding his head. "Oh… Hmmm… okay…" was all Adam could hear from this end of the conversation. "Holy shit! Oh my God, are you kidding me? Do you think I should come right away? Oh, I see… Well, that makes sense, I guess. How is Artie, now? Uh-huh… Uh-uh. Nope…an eyeball! No, I don't think so. Okay. I promise. Love you, too."

"What was that all about," Adam asked, after Tim ended his call and snapped the phone shut.

"Wow, I thought I had shocking news. Don't worry, I wouldn't tell her about Sam being your father. Your *breeder* status satisfied her as *my* big news and your paternity is something Sam can lay on her, not me. I can't imagine she'd be anything but cool with it, though."

"Good, but what's happening in the city?"

"She just finished working the brunch shift and she's gonna stay and work a double, since Artie threw his back out last night."

"But what's the big news?"

"They're finding body parts in the sewers. Jeez! She says this might be a good time for all of us to avoid the Castro, but she also said that Nick would call soon. I guess I'd better drive you back to Hillsborough. I was gonna head south, but my plans are up in the air until I talk to him. He might be calling any minute. Damn, do you know how to make my cell phone ring like a regular telephone? I'm not so much into Beethoven."

"That was Tchaikovsky, but sure."

# Chapter 10

Customers waited in line outside the restaurant on Castro Street. Some were hungry for food and others had no doubt chosen to come to Arts for brunch because of all the juicy gossip. It wasn't every day that human fingers showed up in the sewer pipes. Nick just wanted to finish his omelet and Bloody Mary and be on his way. So he said good-bye to Tim's Aunt Ruth and walked around the corner to Collingwood Street where he'd left his truck. Teresa pulled up in her car at the same time and rolled down her window. "Nick, are you leaving? Will you wait a minute?"

"Sure, Teresa, no problem."

"What luck! Let me just set my groceries inside the gate before I take your parking spot." She pulled her car into the driveway of the apartment building and popped the trunk.

"I'll help you." This was the second time today that Nick volunteered for something and wanted to swallow his words. He was trying to get out of town and instead here he was, facing yet another delay.

"I won't keep you but two shakes, honey. I was dreading the thought of finding a parking spot, but this will work out super!"

Nick saw the enormity of their task before Teresa had even climbed out of the driver's seat. "It seems like Safeway had everything I needed on sale today, so I stocked up."

"Oomph. What have you got in here, bricks?" Nick picked up two of the reusable green fabric grocery sacks and headed for the gate.

"Be careful with those, honey! You must have got the bags with the liquor in them. I tell you what… I'll make us a nice pitcher of Margaritas just as soon as we're done here. You sure deserve one and so do I."

"Thanks, but I've got a lot of driving ahead of me and I already had one of Ruth's Bloody Marys this morning."

"How is my neighbor?" Teresa panted up the stairs behind Nick. "I hardly ever see her at home, lately. She must spend all her time down in Burlingame these days."

"Hillsborough," Nick corrected her.

"Oh, yeah… Burlingame… Hillsborough… whatever… the ritzy suburbs—that's our Ruthie—swimming pools and tennis courts, too rich for my blood, but I can see Ruth fitting in just about anywhere. Good for her."

"She wasn't supposed to come back until tomorrow, but they had some trouble at the restaurant so she drove up this morning to help out."

"Trouble? What kind of trouble?"

"Oh, I don't know. Artie threw his back out and then there was some problem with the plumbing." Nick hadn't meant to tell a lie or be evasive but he didn't want to get stuck here any longer than it would take to haul in the groceries and besides, he'd answered enough questions for one day. "You should ask Ruth and have her tell you all about it."

After three trips up and down the stairs and as many refusals to stay for a drink, Nick got back in his truck and pulled out. He waved and watched in the rear view mirror as Teresa pulled her car into the parking space. He still had plenty of time to see his family in Alameda and drive back to the Russian River long before nightfall. Right now he just wanted to get out of San Francisco and away from the Castro. If he couldn't see Tim there was no reason to be here.

Down in Hillsborough, Dianne got her bags packed, her make-up and eyelashes on, her hair sprayed into an immoveable facsimile of a football helmet, and talked Sam into helping her carry all her bags back out to the car. It took two trips to fill the substantial trunk. "My, you brought a lot with you for just a visit. Your mother always travels so light I don't know how she does it. Last winter in Europe she just had one little suitcase and a carry-on for a two-week trip and she always looked so lovely."

"Have you taken a good look at her lately?" Dianne slid in behind the wheel. "She hardly knows her way around a tube of lipstick. She wouldn't know fashion if it slapped her across the face and that cutesy little pixie haircut of hers—"

"Your mother is beautiful to me."

"—on a woman her age? She gets out of the shower and shakes her head and she thinks she's good to go. I can't imagine going out in public looking like something—"

"Goodbye, Dianne." Sam pushed the car door shut with enough force to block out the rest of her words.

"—the cat dragged in. Sam! Sam?" Dianne looked around and realized her car window was closed and Sam was on his way back to the house. Dianne sniffed and shoved her key into the ignition. She turned the wrong direction out of the driveway and a few minutes later she mistakenly entered the freeway heading south. She was halfway to San Jose before she realized the sun was moving from west to east.

As far as Dianne was concerned, this trip had been one disaster after another. The weekend staff at Sam's estate—what little there was—hadn't been nearly subservient enough for Dianne's taste. Then she couldn't even take a dip in the pool without finding her queer cousin and that colored boy in there. Between the two of them she might have run the risk of catching something. What was worse, she hadn't been able to spend a minute alone with her mother and she really needed to talk to her this time.

Teresa made a pitcher of Margaritas and drank them all by herself. She kept thinking about what Nick said about trouble at the restaurant. She hoped it was nothing serious, but there was only one way to find out. She set her empty glass and pitcher in the kitchen sink and grabbed a sponge to wipe the spilled salt from the little marble table on the back deck. Then she walked over to Arts to get the news straight from the horses' mouths. She figured while she was there she could have a nice visit with her neighbor Ruth, too.

Coincidentally Teresa arrived at Arts at the same time as Dianne and they ended up sitting together at the only open bar stools. Ruth saw them and hurried over. "Teresa, have you met my daughter, Dianne? She's visiting from Texas. Dianne, this is my upstairs neighbor, Teresa. She teaches at the Harvey Milk School just around the corner. What can I get you both?"

"I'll have a glass of dry white wine, mother."

"I'd better stick with a Margarita," Teresa said. "You know what they say, 'never mix; never worry.' How-dya-do, Dianne, what brings you to San Francisco?"

"Why does everyone in this city keep questioning me? Can't I come to visit my own mother without getting the third degree?"

Teresa wasn't sure why this little lady was being so snippy, but she didn't want to get off on the wrong foot with Ruth's daughter. "I didn't mean anything by it. Better take a sip of your wine, honey."

Ruth wrote down her address on Collingwood Street and handed it to her daughter. "My apartment is just around the corner. Nothing fancy, but it's convenient. I hope you'll be comfortable on the couch. I slept there when I came to visit Tim and it was nice and cozy. It's his old apartment, you know. I'll rustle up a set of keys for you as soon as I get… oh, you'll both have to excuse me. Customers are waiting."

Teresa took a generous slug of her Margarita and realized she'd better continue the conversation with Ruth's daughter before awkward silence happened. Teresa hated silence worse than hangovers. "So, how's life down in Texas now that the Bushes have crawled back home to Crawford? Bet you really missed them for eight years, huh?" She laughed, a good, tipsy laugh. "I sure as hell wouldn't! Tell me all about yourself, girl."

The request, and the wine, calmed Dianne; talking about herself was one of her favorite pastimes. "Well, I've been married for sixteen years with two just gorgeous children. Chuck Junior is fifteen—and so tall, he's sure to be a star on the football team—and sweet Barbara is nine. She has her mother's smarts. All A's. Barbara was Miss Junior Texas America when she was only six years old. My husband, Chuck Senior, he works for Standard Oil. Raising a family is such hard work, that I barely have time to keep busy with our local church." She took another deep swallow of her wine. "Oh, yes, I'm secretary treasurer of my collectibles club. Most of the women there, though, well, I could tell you things..."

"Collectibles?" Teresa hid a yawn behind her own glass. "What do you collect?"

"Thomas Kinkade and Danbury Mint... plates and figurines, mostly religious and patriotic items, lots of seasonal things. Christmas is a big holiday for collectibles, as you can imagine, but I love Easter, all those bunnies and ceramic eggs. Some club members frown on them because they don't take into account the religious significance of the holiday, but I think they're darling and I'm going to keep collecting them regardless. We devote time at our meetings to talk about how we can better serve Jesus, of course."

"Oh, Ruthie," Teresa yelled toward the other end of the bar. "That Margarita was fine, but I think I need something stronger now. How 'bout a Martini? And make it a double."

"Coming right up." Ruth worried that Teresa had begun to slur her words. "Didn't you want something to eat too,

Teresa? I could bring you a menu and set you a place right here at the bar. Don't some eggs sounds good, sweetheart?"

Teresa sighed and removed the straw from her glass and licked the last of the salt off the rim. "The only reason I came down here was to hear the dirt. I ran into Nick on Collingwood and he told me there was some trouble down here at the restaurant, but I want it straight from the mortha's house… er… you know what I mean."

"I'd like to see a menu, mother," Dianne said.

"I'll get you both menus." Ruth set the chilled Martini glass in front of Teresa and pretended to get busy at the other end of the bar. She wanted to let the gin melt in the shaker for a good long time so that that it would water down Teresa's drink. She didn't need her daughter Dianne and a drunken Teresa on her hands at the same time. When Ruth came back to the front end of the bar with the menus, she said to Teresa, "So you saw Nick, did you?"

"Now, don't be coy with me, Ruthie." Teresa was definitely slurring. "You know what I'm talking about. What the hell's going on around here?"

The front door opened again and Officer Parker returned. "Hello, Miss Taylor. I was hoping you'd still be on duty. I think I left my pen when I was here earlier."

"Hello there, officer," Teresa turned toward the policeman. "I always like to see a handsome man in a uniform. My name's Teresa, what's yours?"

"Is it the silver one?" Ruth plucked the only pen that didn't have advertising on it out of the jar beside the cash register.

"Officer Parker,' he said to Teresa, "…like the pen. Peter Parker. How do, ma-am?"

"Just like Spiderman, huh?" Teresa used the fingers of her free hand to make a crawling motion up his uniformed shoulder, but he ignored her.

"Thanks, Miss Taylor. That's my pen, alright. I'll need to set up a time to talk to that other fellow too, as soon as possible. I think you said his name was Artie?"

Ruth didn't want to admit that Artie had already come and gone. "I'm sure he'll feel better and be up and about later on in the week. Why not give Arturo a call in a couple of days and he can keep you posted?"

"I also need to compile and check off a list of all the others we want to question. The neighboring businesses on both sides are probably connected to the same plumbing beneath the buildings and we'd like to speak with anyone who has access to that dumpster out back where the items were found."

"But the *items* were only in the dumpster because Nick threw them there after he and Arturo cleaned up the mess from the sewage back-up, right?" Ruth was getting exasperated.

"We can't rule anything out at this stage of the investigation, ma-am."

"Well, the owners of the neighboring businesses should be in on Monday morning to tally the weekend's receipts and go to the bank, I imagine. I don't know anything about the building out in back, though."

"Could you walk me out to my curb, hon?" Teresa stood up and fell into the officer's arms. "I live right around the corner, handsome. Arturo and Artie are across the hall from me, soooo... if you'd help me up my front stairs, I could show you where I live and... and maybe you can talk to him later, honey."

"Artie isn't in any better shape to answer a lot of questions than you are right now. He threw his back out last night."

"Well, I didn't know. I don't know anything that's going on around here. Nick wouldn't tell me. You wouldn't tell me. Maybe Sergeant Porker here will tell me a thing or two. How's about it, handsome?"

"Parker, Ma-am," the policeman said. "Here, let me help you. All I came back for was my pen, actually, and I got it, but it looks like you need a little help there, Miss."

Officer Parker and Teresa had barely got out the door when another of Ruth's neighbors, Marsha, came in and sat down beside Dianne. "How are you today, Marsha?" Ruth asked.

"I'm beat. I just came from my group meeting down at the Center. Could you fix me a tall vodka tonic, please?" Ruth was still thinking about what might happen between Teresa and the policeman, but having Marsha walk in right now meant that Dianne would have a lot to tell her "collectibles" group about when she got home. Ruth set Marsha's drink on a cocktail napkin and got busy with another order at the waiter's station before she could make further introductions.

"Hi, I'm Marsha, Ruth's neighbor," she said to Dianne. "I guess you could say I'm the 'T' in 'LGBT' at the 'LGBT Center' down on Market Street."

"I love your nails. What do you call that color? And pardon my asking, but are they real?"

"They are now. It's Apricot Frost. My hair is real, too. I wore fake nails and wigs for a long time before mine grew out, but now I have my own nails and my hair is long enough to style it just like I want it."

"I'm so sorry, did you have cancer?"

"Cancer! No, what I had was a lot worse than cancer, as far as I was concerned. I had a penis!"

Ruth returned to the front end of the bar in time to say, "Marsha, I see you've met my daughter."

"Your daughter. You're kidding. I didn't know you had a daughter, Ruth. With all that big hair and make-up, I thought for sure she was a drag queen!"

# Chapter 11

Tim didn't sleep nearly as well his second night at Sam's house. He hadn't intended to stay there another night, but when he and Adam got back from their drive, Dianne was gone and the place was just so peaceful he couldn't resist the invitation. He also retained the nagging thought in that back of his mind that there was nothing to go home for.

And Delia had left a hot apple pie on the counter to cool. The smell of warm cinnamon always did him in, a combination of sensory memories of a peaceful place in his early childhood. Had his mother ever been sober enough to bake a pie? Tim doubted it. Maybe his grandmother did or maybe the neighbor who baby-sat him. Most likely it was his Aunt Ruth.

After dinner that night it was just the guys—Tim and Adam and Sam—hanging out and shooting a few games of pool. Tim lost miserably, but realized that it wasn't so bad hanging out with a couple of straight men and getting to know two people he'd soon be related to by Ruth's marriage to Sam. As embarrassed as he was for assuming that Adam was gay, Tim wanted them to become friends. Adam was a great guy, for a straight guy, in Tim's opinion. So was Sam. And Adam's news that Sam intended to propose to Aunt Ruth made perfect sense.

Tim dreamed that night of fire and ice. When it began he was lying on a deck chair beside the pool, just where he'd started out that morning. Adam was nearby. Birds were chirping and flitting about. Then a cloud came over the sun and the sky turned dark. Pink. Orange. Crimson. Black. Tim shivered and rolled over to wrap himself in his towel. The sleek blue surface of the pool turned white. It was a solid sheet of ice and snowflakes started to fall. Tim was bundled up in a parka and mittens and his winter galoshes, staring out at silhouettes of the bare winter trees of Loring Park in Minneapolis. The lake was frozen over and someone had built a snowman in the middle of the lake in the middle of the night. But they'd also built a fire and the snowman was melting.

Tim forgot all about the dream for a while. He drove home to San Francisco on Monday morning and fantasized about his Aunt Ruth and Sam's lavish wedding all the way back to the city. He also forgot about his plans to head south and get away from the city for a while. According to his Aunt Ruth's phone call, something big might be happening in the Castro and he didn't want to miss out on it. Tim could drive down the coast to L.A. another time. He was excited to get back to the city and ready to start meeting with wedding caterers and florists right away.

He drove the Thunderbird from highway 280 up Dolores Street and turned left on 20th. He would have gone directly to the restaurant to find out what was going on, but it was too early. There wouldn't even be anyone there to start setting up yet. He saw a parking spot at the top of Dolores Park, so he took it, got out of the car and spread a towel on the grass. There wasn't much to rush home for with Nick back to work at the nursery. The house on Hancock Street felt emptier than ever. Tim peeled off his shirt, lit a joint and kicked off his shoes. Aunt Ruth said that Nick would be calling him. Why hadn't he? Tim even considered driving up to the river to surprise him, but Tim's stubbornness told him their separation needed to last a little longer. Tim grabbed his cell phone out of his backpack and figured out how to punch in the number. Nick answered on the first ring.

"Hello..."

"Hey, Nick."

"Snowman! How are you? Where are you?"

Tim Snow always loved it when Nick called him "Snowman." It sure beat the dreaded "Snowster" that a previous boyfriend had tried to make stick. No wonder that relationship had been short-lived. "Snowman" invoked some of Tim's few happy memories of childhood winters in Minnesota. Jake once overheard them and thought Nick was talking about cocaine, while crystal meth was a more prevalent drug in the Castro these days... and far more dangerous, in Tim's opinion. The sound of Nick's voice on the phone almost melted away Tim's resolve to maintain their separation a while longer.

"I'm home... well, Dolores Park, actually. Aunt Ruth said you were supposed to call me. What happened?"

"I've been calling you at home. When I got voicemail the first time I called the cell phone. She said you had it with you. I figured you didn't have it turned on and I gave up on trying you that way and I didn't have the number at Sam's."

"I'm calling you on my cell phone right now."

"Where was it last night?"

"Here in my back-pack."

"And where was your backpack?"

"Oh...well... it was in my car, come to think of it... sorry."

"Didn't you notice the messages I left for you?"

"I don't know how to work that part of it yet. Hey, I'll learn, okay? I almost forgot... what was going on at the restaurant? Why did Aunt Ruth have to go back to the city so fast? I know about Artie hurting his back, but she said something about the cops and body parts, too. She didn't go into any detail."

"Wow! It's quite a story. I was gonna try calling you again tonight when I got home from work and tell you all about it then. Man, it's great to hear your voice. So you're finally back in the city?"

"Yeah, just now. Is this a bad time to call? Are you busy?"

"I've always got time for you, Snowman."

Tim smiled and let the sincerity of those words soak in, but he still wasn't ready to submit to his emotions. He was also reminded of the snowman in his dream last night, the frozen lake and the fire. "So, what's going on at Arts?"

"We found fingers in the plumbing. Human fingers… part of a hand. The toilet in the women's room was so backed up that Arturo had to call the plumber in and he ended up tearing the whole floor apart. What a mess!"

"Wait a minute. Back up a little. We? Who's we?"

"Me, actually. I was helping out Arturo. I came down to the city looking for you and I got roped into helping him. Hey, I have to go soon. It looks like the contractor's truck is driving up."

"Wait a minute! What about the fingers?"

"I'll tell you *all* about it later. When can I see you? I'm going crazy, here."

"Soon, I guess. This weekend?"

"I miss you, man."

"How's the new nursery coming along? Was that the contractor?"

"Fine. It's gonna be great. Yeah, he's getting his paperwork out of the back. I've just got a minute. What about you? How are you feeling?"

"I'm okay. I was thinking about taking a long drive down the coast, but I stopped at Sam's place first and my cousin was there."

"The one you don't like?"

Tim groaned. "Don't like. Don't want. An evil rabid Republican right-winger nut-case."

"How did that go?"

"I enjoy torturing her, actually. And Sam has a son I met. Adam. He's black. A fashion model. Really nice, but straight.

Shame, too. Hey, no fair changing the subject. Whose fingers did you find?"

"They don't know yet. The cops are still questioning everybody. Nobody seems to be missing any fingers. So when can I see you, Snowman? Are you still planning to take off on a trip somewhere?"

"I guess not. I spent two nights at Sam's and I was ready to come home. Now that I'm home I didn't even stop at the house. I just came straight to Dolores Park and I'm sitting here staring out at the city like a lovesick fool. I get homesick for San Francisco sometimes."

"Not for me?"

"Aw, aren't you sick and tired of me? You must be, after all this winter of playing nursemaid to an invalid."

"Hell no, Snowman. I was happy I could be there for you. You know... if we could get married in California I'd make those vows to care for you 'in sickness and in health' and all the rest of it and I'd mean every word of them. I even told Jane the same thing. Do you wanna get married, Snowman? We could go to Iowa or someplace."

"Oh, no. Not Iowa. I grew up in Minnesota. That's way too close to home."

"I've really gotta go now. The contractor needs to ask me a bunch of stuff. Can we talk tonight? I'll call you on your cell phone as soon as I get home."

"Sure man... later." Tim didn't want to talk about getting married, anyway. Damn Nick! Just when the conversation was going well, when it felt like things were getting back to normal between them, Nick had to go and bring up a subject like marriage. Damn!

Tim pulled his t-shirt and sneakers back on and tossed the Altoids box back in his bag. Between the sun at the pool at Sam's yesterday and these few minutes in the park this morning without any sun block he was afraid he'd start to burn soon if he wasn't careful. It was time he went home anyway.

...

The bedside phone woke Tim from his nap. He'd been dreaming about the snowman again, but this time it wasn't in Loring Park. It was in San Francisco. Tim couldn't be sure where, exactly, but the fire was raging again and as the snowman melted it revealed a real man underneath. The real man wasn't melting so much as falling apart. Its fingers came off, then its hands and arms. Tim watched another man in black pick up the body parts and pile them into a big green box. No, it wasn't a box; it was a green refrigerator... avocado green. Arms and legs and emerald green eyes went into an avocado green refrigerator on a pea green boat. Now Tim knew where they were. It was China Basin, down by the ballpark. The man in black pulled the cord on the motor and sat down to steer the boat, heading north under the Bay Bridge with his gruesome cargo, heading toward unknown waters on San Francisco Bay.

The phone stopped for a moment and then it started in again. Tim didn't feel like talking to anyone and hoped it would stop on its own, but it was still ringing by the time he'd ambled down the hallway to the kitchen so he picked it up in there. He must have turned off the answering machine.

"How does pot roast sound?"

"Huh? Who is this?"

"Arturo. I called to find out if you want pot roast for dinner. Artie says you're not eating and we're supposed to send food over to your place every night from now on. Your Aunt Ruth said you were back in town, so I was gonna start today."

"How did she find out?"

"Must have talked to Sam... I don't know... maybe Nick. Would you rather have chicken? We've got fresh salmon on the menu tonight, but I'm sure you'll want to heat up whatever I send over. It'll need reheating by the time it gets there and fish is a little more temperamental in the microwave. Would you rather have chicken?"

"I don't need you sending me any food. I'm not an invalid."

"Artie was pretty insistent. I don't want to get on his bad side."

"Let me talk to him."

"He's not here. He threw his back out last night."

"So who's working the bar tonight?" Tim opened the refrigerator and looked inside. There was a carton of strawberry banana yogurt that was well past its "sell by" date, half a loaf of sourdough bread that would make a good doorstop by now, mustard, ketchup, pickles, mayonnaise, grape jelly and a plastic container with a lid. He opened it with one outstretched arm, just in case. It didn't smell, but it was growing enough mold that he didn't recognize its original contents—must have been something Nick left there—and Tim knew it wasn't a Chia Pet. He dumped it down the disposal and set the container in the kitchen sink to soak.

"Your Aunt Ruth and Scott are both working a double."

"I'll come down. Then I can see her and you won't get into hot water with Artie." Tim realized he was getting hungry and he'd either have to go out to eat, go to the store for groceries or dial up something to be delivered. Nick was going to call, but Tim would just have to get used to carrying his cell phone with him.

"You'd better show up by seven or I'll send out the dogs."

"I'll be there by five and I'll eat at the bar so I can visit with my Aunt Ruth. Seeya later then."

Tim closed the refrigerator door and stopped. Something caught his eye. It was the picture of himself and his "date," at Yosemite – the black/Italian guy whose name Tim thought was Mario or Martino. Tim had never seen him again after that trip. He'd moved somewhere back east on a job transfer a week or so later and sent Tim the photograph tucked inside a card the following Christmas. Tim had long ago thrown away the envelope, but he knew the return address was from a cold wintry city where Tim would never want to live year-round. The guy had signed the picture, but the ink was smeared by now and his handwriting was so small and round that Tim had to take the picture down from the refrigerator and hold it directly under the light. It read: "Tim – thanks for a great trip. All best wishes, Bruce."

"Bruce?" Tim said out loud. "Not Mario or Martino or Marcello... Bruce!" Jake had been right all along. Tim was lousy with names, but he never forgot the cock.

It seemed like Ruth had only been home long enough to wash her face and put her feet up for a minute when it was time to go back to Arts and work the dinner shift. "I'm much too old to work doubles, Bart!" she told her cat. "From now on I've simply got to learn when to put my foot down and say no!" She sat down and rubbed her foot instead. The left one. There must have been a pebble in that shoe. "Darn it, it's already time to go."

Ruth had almost crossed Castro Street when she heard a familiar, "Yowl" from behind her. She took three more steps to the curb and turned around to see her cat trundle up and plant himself between her legs with an upturned gaze and another long wail.

"Bartholomew! How did you get out of the apartment? Did you follow me all the way here? To think you crossed Castro Street by yourself... you could have been squished. At least you used the crosswalk, but you don't belong out here in the first place."

Ruth set her purse on the empty newspaper rack and bent down to pick up the cat with both hands. Once he was safely cradled in her left arm she picked up her purse again and glanced at her watch. "Look at the time. I'm gonna be late to work if I carry you back home right now. You bad, bad boy! I don't have time for your nonsense. You're just going to have to come with me to Arts and stay in the kitchen. And you'd better behave yourself. If you get into any trouble in the restaurant Arturo will lock you up in the walk-in pantry until I get a chance to take you home."

...

Tim was the first customer of the evening. He sat at the bar, ordered the fresh grilled salmon, nursed a weak vodka tonic that his Aunt Ruth made for him and then ordered a glass of the house white wine when his dinner came. He looked around the place, listened to people laughing, glasses clinking, knives and forks clattering and realized that he almost missed working here. It was almost time to come back. Almost.

The first forkful of salmon flaked off the filet on his plate and melted in his mouth. Tim missed Arturo's cooking, that was for sure. He was tired of take-out food and Stouffer's dinners and whatever Nick had left behind in unmarked Tupperware containers in the freezer. That was another chore he should tackle this week, defrosting the freezer. What he really wanted to do was buy a new frost-free refrigerator. His was the same one Nick's grandparents had when they lived there, but it still worked.

"How's the salmon?" Ruth asked, but Tim had just taken a second mouthful and she could tell by the look on his face. "I've got to ask Arturo sometime how he does it. I'd love to learn to make salmon for Sam the same way."

"It's incredible," Tim said. "Arturo could give classes… or open a cooking school right here on Castro Street."

Tim came back to Arts for dinner the following night and the next night, too. He told himself it was only to keep people from worrying about him, but at this rate he would soon put on the weight he'd lost and he was almost ready to get back to the gym soon too. Ruth stayed in town that week while Artie's back recuperated, so Tim got to visit with his aunt every night and watch the daily progress on the bathroom remodeling at the restaurant. Both the men's and women's rooms got wider doors with handicapped railings and brand new tile. "We were long overdue to bring them up to code anyway," Arturo said.

Tim was even more interested in the police investigation, which hadn't come as far. One evening Teresa came in while

Tim was eating dinner at the bar. "Hey Tim, how's it going? Mind if I join you? Just a cup of coffee for me, okay? I'm on the wagon."

"What's up with you, Teresa?" Tim was surprised to see his old neighbor not drinking.

"How was your date with Officer Parker the other night?" Ruth asked while she poured a mug of hot coffee and set a basket of sugar packets and a container of half and half on the bar. "Did he walk you home safely?"

"I'll say! I'm surprised you didn't hear us carrying on all the way downstairs at your place. What a night!"

"I was working, remember?" Ruth said.

"Not all night," Teresa said with a smile. "He didn't leave until Monday morning and that was only to go home and change and pick me up again for lunch. We went to that cute little restaurant on Pier 23. Do you know the place? It was a gorgeous day to be down at the waterfront, but man, what a hangover! I wore my darkest sunglasses and I still felt like I might bleed to death every time I opened my eyes. That's when I decided to lay off the booze for a while."

"Are you going to see him again?" Tim asked.

"Peter's working now until Sunday night, but yes, I should think so." Teresa opened her purse to toss her wallet back inside. She threw a dollar tip on the bar when Ruth pushed back the five she had put down for coffee.

"Peter Parker? That's Spiderman's name!"

"Well, that's his name, too and he's as good as any superhero in my book."

"And you met him while he was on the job? In his uniform? Hot."

"Well, technically, he'd only stopped back in to pick up his pen, so it's not as if I was interfering or anything. Then he helped me home. Isn't that a policeman's duty to help drunks and old ladies across the street?

"And right into bed!" Tim laughed. "And you were no doubt drunk, but you're far from an old lady… and I think you're confusing cops with boy scouts."

"But did you find out any more about the investigation?" Ruth quickly tired of listening to their banter when there might be something important to learn.

"Well, they're just about finished..." Teresa began and then stopped short. "I shouldn't tell you a thing, Ruth. I almost forgot I was mad at you!"

"Why would you be mad at me? What did I do?"

"I came down here Sunday night to find out all the gossip and you kept the whole business a secret from me."

"I did not," Ruth said. "I was busy Sunday night with a full bar and besides, I had my daughter here."

"You could have told me something, but no! I had to trade my body and use all of my feminine wiles to coerce the life and death secrets about it from the long arm of the law."

"And you loved every minute of it," Tim said.

"Well yes, but that's beside the point," Teresa said and turned back to Ruth. "How is your darling daughter, anyway?"

"She's a royal pain in the neck, if you must know," Ruth said. "But you didn't hear it from me. I've tried to entertain her as well as I know how, but she is so fussy! I don't know where she gets it. She wasn't brought up that way. Nothing is good enough for her. Everywhere we go she complains about something; she argues with the waiter or waitress. It's so embarrassing! Last night she went to a late movie by herself at the Castro Theatre while I was working. She came here afterward to meet me and she was hungry, but the kitchen was already closed so I took her to Orphan Andy's for a burger and fries."

"Orphan Andy's?" Tim asked.

"I thought she might appreciate some local color. Well, what I really thought was that it might be good to expose her to something outside her usual realm and quite frankly, I was too tired to think of anyplace else nearby that was open late. She sent back her French fries!"

"No," Teresa howled. "At Orphan Andy's?"

"She said they were overcooked. Can you imagine? She acted like she was dining out at the Ritz Carlton or something. Then the whole time we were trying to eat she complained about the movie because people were smoking in it."

"Smoking in the Castro Theatre?" Teresa asked. "What were they smoking? Pot?"

"It was a Bette Davis picture. What in the world did she expect?"

"I should take her to the Nob Hill Theatre," Tim said. "That would give her something to talk about when she gets back to Texas. I don't think they let women in there, though… too bad."

"And then there's another thing…" Ruth said. "I still don't know why she's really here or how long she plans to stay. She always seems to have something on the tip of her tongue that she's about to tell me, but she won't come out with it. She must be miserable sleeping on my couch, considering what she's used to, but strangely enough that's the only thing she hasn't complained about. She sure does like to sleep, though. That's about all she does. Oh, enough about Dianne! Teresa, what else did you get out of Officer Parker?"

"Well, he did this wonderful thing with his tongue between my toes…"

"That's not what I mean and you know it!" Ruth interrupted. "Your body parts can remain your own business! What about the body parts from out back?"

"It's still too early to know very much," Teresa said. "He wanted to question Artie the other night, naturally. He wanted to talk to you too, Tim. Hasn't he called you yet?"

"Me?" Tim asked. "Why me? I haven't been around."

"He said they wanted to get all the information they can from everyone who has worked here. Peter's probably talked to Artie by now, but Artie wasn't answering his door on Sunday night. I didn't give Peter much of a chance to keep knocking, though."

"Haven't you learned anything yet?" Tim asked.

"Peter called me this morning and all they knew was that the fingerprints on the severed hands didn't match any that were on file. The eyeball came from someone who presumably had two of them once and they were green, but no other body parts have turned up so far. There's no match on any missing persons either. They want to question the businesses on either side of Arts and all the present and former employees, so I'm sure he'll be calling you, Tim. He mentioned Patrick, that blond waiter who used to work here until he went off to rehab. There might be something there."

"Jake said he's seen Patrick in the neighborhood lately. Oh, Jake!" Ruth called to him. "Could you come over here a minute?"

"Hi, Ruth. What's up? Hey, Tim."

"You know my neighbor, Teresa, don't you?" Ruth asked.

"Sure… hiya, Teresa."

"We were talking about the police investigation and Patrick's name came up," Ruth said. "I heard you mention that you'd seen him around. Where have you seen him lately?"

"Yeah, I ran into him just this afternoon on Market Street. He was getting a bunch of flyers copied. He's all involved with this new E.T. group. You know Patrick. When he gets involved with something, he goes whole hog. Remember when he was in ACT-UP? He was at a different meeting or demonstration every night of the week. He was always coming in late to work or having to leave early. People think I'm the radical, just because I've got some ink and I'm pierced in a few places. Patrick is the wild one, even though he looks like a Ken doll. I think it was someone in ACT-Up that turned him onto crystal meth. They'd snort a few lines and they could stay up for days planning their next civil disobedience. Then they started shooting it."

"Wait a minute, Jake," Tim said. "Back up. What did you say about E.T.? That's a new one on me."

"Do you mean like 'E.T.,' the extraterrestrial?" Ruth asked.

"E.T., phone home?" Teresa chimed in.

"They use that as one of their slogans, too," Jake said. "Wait a minute. I think I've got a flyer in my bag. Patrick handed me one, not that I'll ever need it. I can show it to you, though."

Jake went to the kitchen and came back seconds later. He set the flyer on the bar between the three of them. "They give these to people coming out of the dance clubs. They have a web site, too, and a 24-hour telephone hot-line."

Tim read aloud, "'*E.T. phone home. Ex-Tweaker Hot Line. Call us whenever you're tempted. No judgments. No questions asked. We've all been there.*' Hmmm..."

"It sounds like a druggie version of that support group they had over at the Most Holy Redeemer Church for heavy drinkers," Teresa said. "Someone tried to get me to go to that once a couple of years ago. That's a laugh! As if I need it – hah!" Tim and Ruth gave each other a knowing look. If anyone was a candidate for rehab it was Teresa, even though she wasn't drinking right now.

"It sure sounds like it," Jake said. "Patrick is in it up to his eyeballs. Sorry... poor choice of words, but it's like this is his new religion."

"I'm glad he's determined to stay off drugs, anyway," Ruth said.

"It's the extremes that bug me," Jake said. "Why can't people just do things in moderation?"

"Like tattoos and trips to the piercing parlor?" Teresa asked.

"Touché, Teresa," Jake smiled. "At least I'm not hurting anybody or doing anything illegal. What does all this have to do with the investigation, anyway?"

"Probably nothing," Teresa said. "The police didn't like the looks of Phil, the piano player, either. Oh, there he is. I forgot he was here this early in the evening. Don't say anything, will you? Peter's going to have his hands full this week with all these interviews. He also said there was something fishy about that guy who just bought the apartment building behind the restaurant, the one that faces onto Hartford Street. He's the brother of the owner of the card shop. They also want to talk to the garbage collectors on that route to ask them about... oh, I've forgotten what it was, now. I think he said something about paint or painting. I had more important things on my mind."

"I'm sure you did, Teresa," Tim said.

"I'll get more out of him Sunday night, I'm sure," Teresa vowed. "Speak of the devil..."

"Officer Parker?" Ruth asked. She had her back to the door and didn't want to spin around to stare.

"No. " Tim chuckled. "Teresa meant the *real* Devil. Delightful cousin Dianne is here."

"Oh, damn..." Ruth said, before she turned around. "Hello Dianne. Are you going to have dinner with us this evening?"

"I don't think I can eat anything, Mother," Dianne whined. "I'm still not recovered from that awful place you took me to last night. Don't you know any nice restaurants in San Francisco?"

"There aren't many in the neighborhood that are open after hours, Dianne, but suit yourself," Ruth tried to remain cheerful.

"Bagdad Café is open all night, isn't it?" Teresa suggested.

"I hear you've become a big Bette Davis fan," Tim needled her. "Is that right, Dianne?"

"Betty who?"

"Bette Davis," Tim said. "Your mother says you went to the Castro Theatre last night to see Bette Davis... the actress... in the movie?"

"Oh, is that who she was?" Dianne scowled. "All I know is the movie was boring. It was so old it was in black and white. The bathroom smelled so musty I wouldn't use it and then these two men started necking right in front of me. It was disgusting. I told them they should get a room somewhere and one of them called me a bitch! I had to move to a different seat. I don't know how much more of this godforsaken city I can stomach!"

"Seeya, Aunt Ruth," Tim said with a laugh. "I'm outta here."

"Thanks for the coffee." Teresa got up from her stool and headed for the door behind Tim.

Ruth looked pleadingly at the two of them as they deserted her. Then the phone rang behind the bar. "Good evening, Arts – Ruth speaking… oh, hello, Sam. No, no, not at all… you couldn't have called at a better time. How are you, dear? That sounds delightful. No, I'm sure Dianne can find some other way to amuse herself for a few hours. She's been quite resourceful, really. I'd love to see you and you can tell me all about it then."

# Chapter 12

Artie finally—reluctantly—agreed to talk with Officer Peter Parker on Thursday afternoon. Amid dramatic sighs and rolling of eyes he admitted, "Why yes, I was tending bar that night when the sewer backed up, but what would I know about plumbing? Nothing! That was the night my back went out… ooh… ouch."

Artie's back was much better now, but he pretended to be exhausted and in pain in hopes that the officer would take pity on him and cut short this grueling questioning. Peter Parker figured he was wasting his time with Artie, anyway.

Friday morning—also on Collingwood Street—Artie ran into Officer Parker again. He was coming down the stairs as Artie was going back up with his morning Chronicle—in his bathrobe! At least Teresa had a smile on her face these days.

Since Artie's back was better he went back to work on Friday night and Ruth got a couple of nights off. On Friday morning she walked from Collingwood over to Tim's place on Hancock for coffee. Even though he'd been in every night this week for dinner, she wanted to spend some time alone with her nephew. "I'm glad you came by," he told her. "All I've done most of this week is watch junk on television and sort through my sock drawer, surf the web, you know…"

"Being cooped up here doesn't sound very healthy, honey."

"I need to get back to the gym or at least start running again. I'd love to go lay out in Dolores Park, but I need to stay out of the sun until I stop peeling. I really overdid it at Sam's pool the other day."

"You have to find something more productive to do than sit around here. Daytime TV will rot your brain. Don't you have anything to read? Did you finish that one about the murderous drag queen? I wanted to borrow it."

"I did and I gave it back to Artie already, but I told him you wanted to borrow it and he said that was fine. You can have it next. He must have forgot. I'll bet it's still at the restaurant."

"I'll ask him. I could bring you Nick's grandmother's new one, *Designed for Death*. I just finished it yesterday. It's set in the New York fashion industry. I bet you'd like it."

"No, I haven't read any of her books yet." The word "fashion" reminded Tim of Adam and he wondered whether Sam had told Ruth yet about him being Adam's biological father, but Tim figured Ruth would have come out with it by now. "How's my dear cousin Dianne getting along? Sorry to abandon you the other night, but there's only so much of her I can take. I don't know how you put up with having her underfoot 24/7."

"Well... Sam has come up with a plan, now that you mention it. He's treating her to a deluxe spa session this afternoon. The only opening they had was at five, which will work out perfectly. She's really going to get the royal treatment... body wrap, deep cleansing facial, manicure, pedicure and hot stone massage. Then she'll have her hair done..."

"You're not sending her to Rene, I hope."

"I wouldn't think of doing that to him. She'll have it done right there in the same place. They have some of the finest stylists and color professionals that will fuss over her like crazy. Sam told the manager to give her the strongest masseuse or masseur they have and tell 'em to really work her over. He wants her so worn out that she'll sleep through the entire weekend. I told him that wasn't necessary because Dianne can always sleep, but Sam feels guilty about stealing her mother away and this should more than make up for it."

"What a waste of money," Tim said. "He could buy her a bottle of some fruity bubble bath and a fresh spray can of Aqua Net and she'd be just as happy."

"It might do her good. Sam gave me a spa treatment for my birthday and I felt wonderful for days afterward. At least she won't find anything to complain about there."

"Are you sure?"

"No reasonable person would," Ruth sighed and frowned. "I forget sometimes that she's in a whole different category from reasonable. Anyway, it will give Sam and me an evening alone and most of tomorrow together. I've got an appointment with Rene to have my hair done today at two o'clock. I called Mai Ling yesterday and she said he had a cancellation, someone famous. Mai Ling couldn't tell me the name, but she sounded terribly disappointed. I'll have to scour the papers tomorrow. There was nothing in Leah Garchik this morning and she doesn't have a column on Saturdays, but she's more apt to cover that after the fact than beforehand. You know... a sighting. Oh my, look at the time. I've got to get going."

"Where's Sam taking you?"

"We're spending the night at the Claremont Hotel in the Berkeley Hills. But we don't want anyone else to know, okay?"

"You don't want anyone else to know where you are or you don't want anyone else to know that you and Sam are sleeping together?" Tim asked.

"That's right, dear... see you later."

Ruth had left her car in such a good parking spot on Collingwood Street that she decided to take MUNI downtown for her hair appointment. She could also save a few dollars by not having to pay for parking in the Union Square garage. A trip to Rene's salon was a big expense by Ruth's Midwestern standards. Besides, she'd rather spend the money on tips for Mai Ling and the new girl, the one who washed her hair. Ruth caught the F-Line streetcar next to the Twin Peaks bar, rode down Market Street to Powell and walked uphill from the cable car turnaround the few blocks to Sutter.

"Thanks for squeezing me in on short notice, Rene. I always feel so much better after I've seen you. Having you work your magic is almost as good as a massage and an hour on an analyst's couch all rolled into one."

"How you talk, Miss Ruth! You know I can always find time for my favorites and besides, Miss Timmy wouldn't let me hear the end of it if I let you get too scraggly-looking."

Ruth always laughed when she heard Rene refer to her nephew as "Miss Timmy," but that was just his way and she was getting used to it by now, just like so many other things. A couple of years ago in Minneapolis she never would have imagined that her marriage—on life-support for so many years—would finally give up the ghost. She'd tried hard to make things work out with Dan, but some painful things were meant to be. Getting through them meant coming out the other side of the ordeal with a rosier outlook and a brighter future than ever.

She never would have imagined she'd meet a man as wonderful as Sam, either... or end up bartending on Castro Street and turning into a token mother-figure for dozens of gay men. That's how she felt about most of her customers, too... well, most of the time. And she never would have dreamed she'd be sitting here in Rene's salon off Union Square in San Francisco, listening to him talk about "Miss Timmy" while he snipped away at her split ends and turned her around and around in the chair.

"I heard you had a cancellation... someone famous?"

"Now where on earth would you hear a thing like that, Miss Ruth?"

"Mai Ling told me when I called. She said you had a cancellation and she sounded so disappointed, didn't you, Mai Ling? I thought it must have been a movie star."

Rene let out a laugh and Mai Ling lifted the nail file from Ruth's right foot and looked up at her with an expression that was something between a glare and a grimace. Ruth gasped and said, "Oh, no… am I speaking out of turn? I didn't mean to get you in any trouble, Mai Ling, honestly."

Rene shook his finger at his employee, but kept on smiling. "So much for confidentiality, Mai Ling. What have I told you about babbling away like a magpie? Shame on you!"

"Who was it?" Ruth asked. "Now I'm dying to know."

"Who was it, Mai Ling?" Rene taunted. "Go ahead and tell Miss Ruth about your idol cancelling her appointment."

Mai Ling dropped the nail file, covered her face with both hands and ran out of the room. Ruth said, "Now look what we've done. I feel terrible about it, Rene. I'm so sorry."

"It serves her right for blabbing. That girl needs to learn to not go telling folks things. Sally, the new girl, the one that washed you out… she was the one that took the reservation in the first place, and I don't want her picking up any of Mai Ling's bad habits. You know I'm not one to gossip, Miss Ruth. If people thought their secrets weren't safe with me, they wouldn't feel near as comfortable coming to see me, you know."

"But now you've just got to tell me her name, at least."

"You probably don't even remember Miss Nancy Kwan, do you?"

"From *The World of Suzie Wong*? Of course I remember her. I didn't know she was coming to town. I haven't thought of her in years."

"Whenever I hear her name mentioned, I think of *Flower Drum Song*. You know the one where she sang 'I enjoy being a girl.' It's kind of a camp classic with the drag queens, or at least it used to be. And she was also known for that famous bob haircut. Miss Vidal Sassoon gave her that cut personally. Oh-me-oh-my! Mai Ling idolizes that woman!"

"And don't forget her TV commercial for Pearl Cream," Ruth said.

"Ancient Chinese secret!" Rene laughed.

"So is Nancy Kwan a regular client of yours when she's in San Francisco?"

"Hell no! Like I said… Sally took the reservation and Mai Ling couldn't read her handwriting. It was Nancy Kahn, a nice wealthy widowed lady from Pacific Heights. She comes in every few weeks and she had to change it to next Tuesday at the last minute, so I had more room for you, Miss Ruth. But don't you fret… I would have fit you in, anyway."

"Poor Mai Ling," Ruth said.

"It serves her right. If anyone is going to do the gossiping around here, it'll be *moi* and you know I'm not one to gossip."

Ruth laughed, but she still felt sorry for Mai Ling and slipped her an extra five dollar bill on her way out of the salon. She'd saved at least that much by not parking in the Union Square garage.

Coming home afterward, Ruth splurged on a cab ride to the corner of 18th and Castro. She still had plenty of time before Sam came by to pick her up and she needed a few things at Walgreens. She walked up Castro Street toward home with her purse in one hand and her Walgreens bag in the other and heard a woman's voice calling out her name. "Ruth… oh, Ru-uth!"

She didn't see anyone at first and then noticed a lady climbing out of a cab in front of Arts with a sea of shopping bags. It was Nick's grandmother, Amanda Musgrove. Ruth waved and looked both ways, stepped between two parked cars and jaywalked across Castro Street in the middle of the block. The lady driver of the #24 Divisadero bus heading south tooted her horn and waited. Ruth recognized her as a customer from Arts and waved her thanks. Soon she was exchanging pecks on the cheek with the elderly mystery writer as her cab pulled away. "How nice to see you, Amanda. What brings you to San Francisco?"

"I was downtown shopping and then I'd hoped to see you for a refreshing afternoon cocktail. It must be five o'clock somewhere. What are you doing out here instead of working behind the bar?"

"It's my night off, but Artie can make you one... or Scott."

"That's alright, dear," she said with a frown. "Nick's father, my son, is doing some boring business at his lawyer's and I finished my shopping, but I really wanted to see you. Nick told me about the events of last weekend." Amanda peered into the window of the video store next-door to the restaurant as if she were looking for clues.

"It's just past five o'clock. Let's go inside and talk. I have plans with Sam this evening, but I can spare an hour or so." They went inside and Ruth reintroduced Mrs. Musgrove to Scott the bartender. "Do you want your usual, Amanda? A rye Manhattan?"

"No, thanks... that can wait. Tell me what's been going on around here. Have the police discovered anything yet?"

"Nothing for me either, Scott... maybe later." Ruth turned back to Mrs. Musgrove. "If they've found anything, they haven't told us about it yet. We have sort of a mole, though. My neighbor Teresa has latched on to one of the investigators on the case. She says they haven't ruled out anything or anyone, but they suspect that the piano player might be involved. Poor Phil, just because he's so good looking people always want to blame him for everything."

"What do you say you and I have a look around?" Amanda suggested.

"You want to look in the dumpster where they found the hand?" Ruth asked.

"Well, you know your way around here better than I do. Yes, let's start in the back of the restaurant and then I think we should have a look at that apartment building behind here. How is your nephew, by the way?"

"Tim's okay. It's time for him to get back to work soon. I think he's getting bored at home with Nick not around as much." Ruth led Amanda through the kitchen, "Now this is the door to the back and there's the dumpster where your grandson was tossing the buckets of sludge on Sunday morning. It's been emptied since then, of course."

"And that's the back door of that apartment building," Amanda pointed, "with a heavy padlock. Isn't that odd? I should think the fire marshal would discourage blocking the alternate exit."

"I'm sure he would, that is... if anyone were living there. I heard they were remodeling the apartments, something about turning them into condos."

"Let's walk down the driveway and have a look at the front."

"I'm sure that's locked too. I don't see anyone working today."

They both stopped and looked up at the side of the building. A window opened on the top floor and they could hear the sound of a faucet being turned on, then the spray of a shower and the banging of pipes in the walls. "I have an idea, Ruth. Do you know where we could find a few old newspapers or magazines?"

"On the shelves between the rest rooms... there are the *B.A.R.* and *Bay Times* and *maybe* some of those smaller glossy ones," Ruth said. "They're all free. Why do you ask?"

Amanda reached inside her purse and pulled out two copies of *Watchtower.* "Can you find about a dozen papers this size?"

Ruth went inside and came right back out with the papers. Amanda took half of them and gave Ruth the rest, placing a copy of Watchtower on top of each stack. "Now... here, tie this scarf over your head. You look a little too nice with your hair freshly done to be a Jehovah's Witness."

"We'll never get away with this. I don't know anything about their beliefs or their practices or what to say if—"

"You won't have to say anything," Amanda assured her. "If it comes to that, you just let me do all the talking, but I doubt that will even be necessary."

Ruth tied the black scarf over her head, picked up her stack of papers once again and followed her friend down the driveway. When they reached the front door, Amanda put a black scarf over her own head and rang all of the doorbells, one at a time. At last, the buzzer sounded to open the gate and she grabbed it, slipped a newspaper inside and let it close again on the paper. She stepped back again and rang the same bell repeatedly, the only one that had elicited any response. Someone finally opened a front window on the top floor. A man with a towel on his head hollered down, "Is that you, Eddie? Whatsamatta? I said six o'clock, damnit! You're early. Hey! Who the hell are you broads? Go away! We don't need none 'o 'yer religion crap!"

Amanda grabbed Ruth by the elbow and pulled her up the street away from the apartment building until the man put his head back inside and closed the window. "We're in luck," she said. "He's the only one home and he's on the top floor. Let's have a look inside."

They pulled off their scarves and went back to the gate that Amanda had propped open. They left both stacks of gay newspapers on the bottom step and Amanda put the *Watchtower* papers back in her purse. "You never know when these might come in handy."

"Now what?" Ruth asked.

"Did you recognize that guy?"

"I couldn't get a good look at him between the towel over his face and the scarf over most of mine, but I don't think so. I didn't recognize his voice, anyway."

"Good, then he's no one you know." Amanda led the way through the downstairs hallway toward the rear of the building. They were just inside the door that was padlocked from the outside. "Something smells funny down here, doesn't it?"

"Yes, it's almost like a sweet, sort of chemical smell. It's not your typical damp cellar odor of mildew and it doesn't smell like laundry deter—"

"Meow!" came the loud cry of a cat as it leapt down from a water heater and landed in Ruth's arms.

"Bartholomew! Where have you been? I thought you were hiding under the bed this morning. How did you get all the way over here? You bad boy." Ruth held the cat and petted him for a moment until he jumped down and scampered through a hole in a corner of the room. "I can't believe it. That's my cat I dragged all the way out here from Minnesota. He's become more and more scarce ever since my daughter arrived. He can't stand her!"

Amanda pulled a small flashlight out of her purse and pointed it in the direction where the cat had disappeared. The wall there was old wainscoting with chipped yellow paint. "The smell is even stronger over here." She ran her black-gloved hand along the dirty trim of the boards. "Hold this flashlight, Ruth. Aim it right along here while I try pushing on these boards."

The panel popped open to reveal another room where the cat had gone, but there was no sign of Bartholomew now. Ruth sprayed the flashlight's dim beam around the dark room. It wasn't strong enough to reach the far corners, but the women could see that the floor was littered with antifreeze containers and empty Drano cans. A trash barrel overflowed with used coffee filters stained red. Along the nearest wall stood an assortment of camping fuel cans and a dozen half-gallons of paint thinner.

"Paint!" Ruth said. "That was the other thing Captain O'Sullivan asked us about that I forgot. He wanted to know if anyone had been painting in the restaurant because they found a bunch of paint cans in the dumpster.

"Are you sure you heard him say that they found paint *cans*?" Amanda asked.

"No, come to think of it... they might have said paint thinner."

"Meow!"

"Bartholomew? Where are you, boy?" Ruth turned the flashlight toward the back of the room where they discovered that it opened in an L-shape to reveal an even larger space. Ruth froze in her tracks. The stench was even worse here.

Amanda took the flashlight from Ruth and stepped further inside. One large wooden table held a hot plate and enough vials and beakers to be the envy of any junior high school science wiz. "Ruth, come here and take a look at this."

Ruth didn't want to go any further. She wished she had a flashlight of her own and she sensed that she had seen enough for one day. "I can't see anything and this place gives me the creeps." Ruth wanted to run back out into the sunlight, but she heard her cat again.

"It's a regular laboratory," Amanda said. "And there's another table too. It has some knives on it and it looks like—"

Ruth screamed, "Bartholomew! What are you doing?" The cat was perched high on an old wooden chopping block. He was licking something shiny and wet off a meat cleaver. "My God, Amanda… that looks like blood. I'm sure it's blood! Let's get out of here."

"I think I could use that Manhattan about now. Let's go back to the restaurant and call the police."

# Chapter 13

Tim woke up early on Saturday morning. He was naked and sweaty, his legs tangled in a knot of damp sheets that he tried to kick off as he came out of his dream. He opened his eyes and noticed the dim light of dawn on the misty bedroom windows. He'd been having one of his *important* dreams—he just knew it—but as soon as he opened his eyes it slipped away. He squeezed his eyes shut tight again, tried not to move, tried not to breathe, tried to hold onto it, but it scurried away like roaches in the light.

He'd been having psychic dreams for years, just like his late grandmother did, or so they told him. He could barely remember her, but still kept her picture on his nightstand, a framed photograph of Tim as a small boy beside her on a blue and green plaid blanket by the lake in Powderhorn Park in Minneapolis on the Fourth of July. He looked at the picture again as he rolled over to the dry side of the bed. He wished his grandmother could answer all his questions and help him now. *What good are these dreams? They're only a nuisance if I can't figure out what they mean. And now I'm having night sweats again? Do I need to see my doctor again and have him change my meds? Why am I burning up tonight? Why did you leave me with this stupid, so-called gift when I don't know what to do with it?*

All that Tim could remember about the dream had to do with a fire, a huge hot conflagration, with flames shooting high into the sky above the treetops. Maybe the fire had already happened. Sometimes Tim's dreams worked that way. He was in the hospital in Sebastopol last winter when Nick's nursery and greenhouses exploded, sent showers of glass through the redwood trees, collapsed in upon themselves and burned to the ground. *No… this fire hasn't happened yet… and it will be right here in San Francisco… right here in the neighborhood… and it will be close enough that I can smell it.*

Tim woke up again an hour later. He put on the coffee and ran down the front steps for the morning paper. The Saturday Chronicle was as thin as a supermarket flyer these days, now that the Internet had killed the want-ads and there was apparently no real news this week. He checked his email and discovered a note that Nick had sent late last night:

> *Hey, Snowman. I won't call you because it's pretty late and I'd hate to interrupt your beauty sleep, but I'm coming down to the city tomorrow afternoon and I hope you'll want to see me. This separation has gone on long enough, as far as I'm concerned. Can I take you to dinner? Let me know what you think. Otherwise I'll drive straight to Alameda to my folks' house. I want to see you bad, man!*

Tim hit REPLY and sent a one-word response:

> *Cum!*

He'd thought all week that he needed more time alone or that Nick needed more time alone, but now that he'd made up his mind about it, Tim couldn't wait to see Nick again. He knew he should stay out of the sun, but he decided to head to Dolores Park this morning anyway. He needed the walk and the fresh air would do him good. He lathered on a thick coating of sun block as soon as he got out of the shower.

He hoped he'd made the right decision. He hoped that Nick wasn't coming to see him out of pity. Tim could always find something to be paranoid about, but now his physical craving to be with Nick outweighed any other factors.

There was barely a breeze in the park and the only clouds in sight were fleecy cotton balls nudging the towers of the Bay Bridge. It was already getting crowded, even for a Saturday, but Tim had noticed lately that weekdays could be just as busy if the weather was good. San Franciscans weren't apt to let little things like going to work get in the way of a perfect day. Tomorrow might be foggy or "the big one" might hit tonight.

"The big one" meant the next big earthquake to most people, but the first time Tim heard that expression was on Castro Street, so he just assumed someone was bragging about his new boyfriend or his latest trick. Tim crossed the footbridge over the MUNI tracks and the sound of bongo drums floated up. He looked down over the railing and spotted the source, a sexy brown-skinned boy with hair past his shoulders. It was strung with feathers and beads and Tim thought at first that the boy was naked. It was hard to tell, considering the strategically placed drums and the way his hair fell. He was a photograph from another time.

Tim spread a towel on the "gay beach" below 20th and Church Streets. It was too early for the ice cream vendors' carts. Their bells reminded Tim of his first tricycle, but the only sounds now were from a helicopter over the freeway and distant sirens. This morning's dream tried to creep back into his memory... something about guns and the police. The fire came later on. If only Tim's grandmother had lived long enough to teach him what these dreams were for... if only she'd explained to him the specialness, the "gift"—as they called it—that rare talent that belonged to him now.

Police and guns were nothing extraordinary. Cops carried guns. So what? Tim's frustration made him disgusted with himself and his useless dreams. It was still before noon, but he fished the Altoids box out of his backpack and took two hits off a fresh joint. Then he pulled out the Thermos of coffee and the newspaper.

Tim hadn't believed his downstairs neighbor Jane when she said they might close Dolores Park for two years, but here was an article about it. How could they? This was like Tim's back yard. Sure, the toilets needed repairs and the playground could stand to be modernized, but two years? The whole park? It had something to do with Obama's stimulus package for shovel-ready projects. What could be more shovel-ready than a former cemetery? Tim thought about writing a letter to the White House threatening not to vote for Obama in 2012 if they closed Dolores Park for two full years!

He was supposed to be looking for something else in the paper. What was it his Aunt Ruth had told him? Oh, yeah... she got in to see Rene to have her hair done yesterday because some movie star had cancelled. Tim flipped through the Chronicle, but he didn't see mention of any movie stars. Leah Garchik might have had something about it in her column, but she only ran Mondays through Fridays. No matter. What did Tim care about movie stars? Nick was coming down tonight.

It might be more practical to send an email to his local supervisor, or was Bevan Dufty too busy running for mayor these days to worry about Dolores Park? A J-Church streetcar stopped on the corner and a gaggle of 20-something gay boys got out, mincing and giggling toward where Tim was sitting. They plopped down blankets a few yards away and started blasting their music, if you could call it that. Hip-hop wasn't what Tim had in mind today. It was common knowledge that Bevan Dufty was Billie Holliday's god-son. At least Billie sang songs with understandable lyrics. What would she think about a generation of young gay white boys playing black music that wasn't really music and wasn't really poetry? Now Tim was in one of his indignant moods and even more convinced that he should write to Bevan Dufty. Something had to be done!

Tim took another hit off the joint and turned to the crossword puzzle, but it was a tricky one today. The New

York Times Sunday puzzle was always in the Chronicle the following Saturday. Tim got a few of the smaller words before he got stuck on six down… six letters… "place." Sometimes it helped to put it aside for a while. Maybe it was a verb, not a noun. He was tempted to call Aunt Ruth to see if she'd finished this one yet. She was so good at crosswords and his cell phone was somewhere in his backpack. Then he remembered she was with Sam. They would be waking up in their suite at the Claremont this morning.

"Tim Snow!" Someone shouted. "Over here! Hey… Tim!" A blond guy on a bicycle stopped on the sidewalk, climbed off and came toward him. The noise of a J-Church streetcar heading south blocked out any other sound for the moment.

"Hiya Patrick," Tim recognized his co-worker—his *former* co-worker. Tim hadn't seen Patrick in months, since long before Tim's accident. He tried to remember when. It must have been back when he and Patrick were both still working at the restaurant before Patrick went off to the Betty Ford Clinic. Was that the first or the second time?

"Looking good," Tim said. Patrick had put on a few pounds in the right places and lost that hollow-cheeked look he was showing toward the end. "What's new?"

"Haven't you heard?"

Tim didn't know what Patrick meant, but he tried to be subtle about hiding the Altoids box under his Chronicle. "Heard what?"

"Well, for starters, I've been clean and sober over six months this time," Patrick announced.

Whenever Tim heard the words "clean and sober," he craved a cold beer or a salty Margarita more than a joint. "Congratulations… but what do you mean 'this' time?"

"Well, it didn't happen overnight. Arturo and Artie sent me to the Betty Ford Clinic the first two times, you know…"

"No, I didn't," Tim said. "I thought—"

"But that didn't take," Patrick shook his head, paused and looked away for a moment, staring off across the Dolores Park before he continued. "I met a really sweet guy at Betty

Ford, though – Darryl. We hit it off, sorta became boyfriends, and when we both got out I spent a few weeks with him in Santa Monica. It was the first time either one of us had ever had sex without being high on something."

"Ever?" Tim liked to smoke pot before sex, but he couldn't imagine that he'd never had sex when he was "clean and sober".

"First time in years, anyway. We only tried it once though – straight, I mean. Then we both got so turned on—after all that dry time—we just had to get high so we could keep on going."

Tim thought Patrick might be clean and sober now, but he still talked like a speed freak. Tim could barely manage to get a word in when Patrick stopped to breathe. "Oh Patrick..." Tim said. He was frowning now, but at least he'd managed to get two words in together this time – "Oh" and "Patrick."

"Haven't you ever fucked on crystal, man?" Patrick asked.

"No I haven't and I'm not into partying... just pot."

"Well, don't knock it until you've tried it! You can do amazing things and you can go for days and days." Patrick stopped and said, "Sorry. That's the old tape playing. That was the 'old' Patrick. I don't do that anymore. I don't need to. I'm better than that."

"It sounds like—" Tim tried again.

"Now I work with E.T. That stands for 'Ex-Tweakers.' A lot of the guys from Tweaker.org moved over to this group. They took all they'd learned there and put a new spin on it and now we're really helping people get clean. It's given my life a whole new meaning. Last night I was out South of Market all night long. Lots of partiers down there. We handed out flyers until they closed the dance floor and we talked to people who wanted help coming down, let them know about us. Tonight I'm working Collingwood Park."

"What about Darryl?" Tim asked. "What happened to—"

"He moved back up here with me. I haven't seen him in a couple of weeks, though. He went to Santa Barbara for his grandmother's funeral and then he was gonna look up some old friends."

"I hope he's—"

"Tim, how are *you* doing, anyway?" Patrick asked. "I heard all about your Aunt Ruth discovering the big meth lab in the Castro yesterday afternoon."

"What?" Tim sat bolt upright on his beach towel.

"Haven't you heard?" Patrick asked while Tim reached into his backpack again, bypassing the Altoids box and groping for his cell phone. He still wasn't sure how to work all its gadgetry, but between Nick and his Aunt Ruth, they had taught him the basics, like how to call either of them whenever he needed to. If he'd known he could access dudesurfer.com from his cell phone, he would have learned all its features a long time ago.

*"Hi! You have reached Ruth Taylor's voice mail. Please leave me a message at the…"*

"Damn," Tim said to Patrick, as well as to the phone in his hand. "She must be—"

"I'm surprised she didn't tell you, of all people," Patrick said. "It was in that apartment building on Hartford that just got sold. You know the one right behind the restaurant."

"Behind Arts?" Tim asked.

"Yeah, she was with some other older lady. She was the one who actually called the cops because your Aunt Ruth had to be someplace. Maybe that's why she didn't call you." Patrick glanced at his watch. "The news was all over South of Market last night, though. Man, look at the time. I've gotta go. It was good talking to you. Take care, okay?"

Patrick was up and away on his bicycle, pedaling down the sidewalk in the direction of Mission High School before Tim could even find his lighter. He took a long toke off the joint and tried the phone again. *"Hi! You have reached Ruth Taylor's…"* It was Saturday. Arts would be open for lunch. He could walk over there and find out what was going on. Artie would know or Arturo would be able to tell him.

Tim dropped the phone into his bag and leaned back on his beach towel. There was no big rush. It wasn't even noon yet. There was a slight breeze and this was the first time he had smoked grass since last weekend at Sam's pool when he met Adam. He'd gotten out of the habit this winter while he was wrapped in a cast and bandages, afraid it would make his claustrophobia worse.

He wriggled his toes and stretched out his arms and legs and took another hit. Nick was coming to town this afternoon and Tim would get to spend the evening and the whole night with him and all day Sunday. It would be just like old times when they first met. Tim realized he felt better than he had in a long time.

Distant laughter floated on the breeze over the crest of the grassy ledge where Tim had spread his things. He sat up and listened, poured another cup of coffee from the Thermos and picked up the crossword puzzle. Maybe being stoned would help him see the clues in a new light. Tim heard one laugh that curled up into a tiny squeal at the end. He knew that laugh; it was Sarah, the downstairs neighbors' daughter, the magic child. Tim shielded the sun from his eyes with his hand.

Sarah was on a swing moving in tall arcs through the air. She was being pushed by a handsome black man… it had to be Adam, of course, but Tim didn't recognize him right away with all his clothes on. They had spent more time together in swimsuits beside Sam's pool in Hillsborough or riding bare-chested in the Thunderbird convertible with the top down than they had with their clothes on.

It took Tim another moment to remember that Adam was Sarah's uncle. Tim wondered when Adam had arrived in San Francisco but he was too stoned now to ask him. His brain was spinning with thoughts of his Aunt Ruth discovering a meth lab behind the restaurant, his big date with Nick this evening and knowing he shouldn't stay out in the sun too long. It was odd that he should run into Patrick today, too.

Tim's brain reeled with a thousand jumbled thoughts. Maybe Patrick knew what was going on, if only he didn't talk so fast. Maybe there was something to be said for being "clean and sober" now and then, after all. Tim glanced back down at the Chronicle crossword. Six down... six letters... place... "locate" would fit.

Then the fiery dream started coming back and Tim wondered if he was too stoned to walk down to the playground and say hello.

# Chapter 14

When Tim arrived at Arts that afternoon, Teresa was alone at the bar. She was the only person he knew in the place besides Artie and neither he nor Teresa noticed Tim come in. Teresa's focus was in the palm of her hand and Tim realized she must be texting someone. He was still getting used to his cell phone and couldn't understand why so many people these days were happy to have their attention so far away from where they were. Teresa was put together better than usual, especially for a Saturday. She had on a pale green blouse that matched her slacks and her blonde hair was pulled back away from her face. Tim thought she might even be wearing make-up.

Three 20-something dykes—two of them with tattoos and spiked hair—took up the stools near the front door. Tim remembered them from months ago when they'd had dinner in his section. Surprisingly good tippers, if he remembered right. Teresa was at the middle of the bar with several empty stools on either side of her.

"Hi Teresa… mind if I join you? You look like you're busy."

"Hey, Tim." She jumped a bit, put away her Blackberry and turned toward him. "Sit yourself down. It was just my sister in Seattle. She wants me to go in with her on a birthday present for mom."

"What are you drinking?"

"It's coffee. I'm on the wagon

"You're *still* on the wagon? Did hell freeze over or what?"

"Shut up, you!" Teresa slapped his knee. "This is not a permanent situation. It's just that I've got a new man in my life and I thought it might be nice to remember in the morning what we did the night before. There's nothing wrong with that, is there?"

"The cop, you mean? No, there's nothing wrong with that at all. And I'm in no position to judge anyone else."

"I never thought of you as a big drinker."

"I'm not... usually... but this morning I smoked a joint in Dolores Park and I can still feel it. I must be out of practice; it'd been a while. I got home from the park and took a shower and I was so stoned I was still standing there after the hot water ran out... brrr!"

At the end of the bar near the kitchen, a pair of pink fruity drinks in fancy glasses stood in front of a couple of strangers—tourists, no doubt. Artie pulled out the San Francisco street map from beside the cash register, moved their drinks to either side and spread the map across the bar. They laughed about something Artie said, but Tim and Teresa didn't catch the joke. Tim was always amazed at how smooth Artie was. He could be so charming and funny, even when he wasn't in drag.

"So... Teresa... where's that cop of yours?"

"Peter's out back with Captain O'Sullivan."

"Aha! So *that's* why you're sitting here drinking coffee. Don't lie to *me*! You don't want him to catch you falling down drunk at the bar."

"Shut up! That's exactly how we met, now that you mention it... when I was falling down drunk at the bar." Teresa laughed. "They've got their whole team back there dusting for fingerprints, spraying Luminol all over the place."

"What's that?" Tim asked.

"Luminol? Don't you watch the cop shows? It shows blood in places where you can't see it with the naked eye. Peter figures that the building out back is where the fingers they found in the pipes must have come from, so they're treating it as a crime scene. You didn't hear a word of this from me though, alright? Promise me, Tim!"

Artie glanced up from the map and looked over at Tim for the first time since he walked in. "Hey there, stranger. When did you get here? Are you ready to come back to work yet?"

"Soon, Artie, soon."

"You wanna drink?" Artie asked, but he didn't move from his spot in front of the tourists, elbows on the bar with one foot propped up on a beer box.

"No thanks, but hey... Artie, what's all this about my Aunt Ruth discovering a meth lab? And now Teresa tells me there's a murder investigation going on out back, huh?"

"I did *not* tell you that! You stinker!" She gave him another playful slap. "Well, at least now you can see what happens when I'm sober enough to pay attention. The next thing I need to learn is how to keep my mouth shut."

"Now's the time to buy you a drink! I'll get you to spill it all!" Tim laughed. "Can I get you something Teresa... really?"

"I'm tempted... but no... I better wait until Peter's finished and find out what his plans are. He was supposed to be off today. Hey, have you talked to your Aunt Ruth or how did you hear about this?"

"From Patrick, the one who used to work here," Tim started. "Artie, you should hear this, too. Come here and I can start over. I ran into Patrick this morning in Dolores Park. He told me about Ruth and some other lady..."

"Amanda Musgrove," Teresa filled in.

"I would have guessed as much," Tim said.

"Do you mean *our* Patrick?" Artie budged from his comfortable position and moved toward them. "Our old waiter, Patrick?"

"Speed freak Patrick, you mean," Tim nodded.

"He's not using that stuff again, is he?" Artie asked. "Arturo will be so disappointed after all the... well, you know."

"Yeah, he told me how you guys helped him out. The Betty Ford Clinic isn't cheap! Patrick told me all about it and... No, he swears he's been... whatchamacallit... 'clean and sober' for six months this time. The way he brags about it made me want a drink! He still talks like a speed freak, though. I could hardly get a word in edgewise."

"He always talked fast, didn't he?" Artie asked.

"I don't think so, Artie. Not to that extent. Anyway, he told me it was all over town about Ruth and some old lady finding the meth lab in the building behind here. I guess Patrick doesn't know Nick's grandmother."

"That reminds me," Teresa said. "You might want to warn your Aunt Ruth and Mrs. Musgrove that O'Sullivan is furious at both of them for getting involved in police business."

"I would think he'd be grateful they discovered the scene of the crime. The police weren't having much luck on the case and it was only yards from where we're sitting right now."

"I told him Ruth was just looking for her lost cat," Artie said. "I told him she heard Bartholomew meowing out by the dumpster and followed him. Ruth says he's been miserable ever since your cousin came to town."

"I can't blame the poor cat for running away from Dianne!" Tim said.

"O'Sullivan is also pissed that Ruth slipped out before he arrived," Teresa said. "Mrs. Musgrove was the one who called the cops and filed the report. They want to question Ruth but all they get is her voice mail."

"Same here, but she's still shacked up with Sam at a fancy hotel in the East Bay," Tim said. "I wouldn't answer either. But why does this cop need to talk to Aunt Ruth if Mrs. Musgrove answered all their questions?"

"I think he just wants to put the fear of God in her," Artie said. "He couldn't intimidate Nick's grandmother and he feels like the ladies are showing him up."

Tim turned toward Teresa. "What does Peter have to say about it?"

"About what? O'Sullivan? Or the ladies?"

Before Tim had a chance to continue, the front door opened and the doorframe was filled with the silhouette of a tall black man. "Adam!" Tim stood up and went to the door to shake hands. "Welcome to Arts!"

He had a woman with him, a slim and elegant woman. It wasn't every day that such a stunning creature descended onto Castro Street, a *real woman* wearing a dress. Adam touched her arm and shoulder with his hands and moved behind her. The peach-colored fabric clung to her perfect figure and the skirt shimmered slightly as she walked. Tim knew right away that this wasn't a drag queen.

"Tim, I'd like you to meet my fiancée, Alexandra."

"Oh, wow!" Tim shook hands with both of them. "I thought you looked familiar. I've only seen you in pictures in magazines, but you're even more beautiful in person. It's nice to meet you, Alexandra."

"Thank you. I've heard nice things about you too. But please call me Alex."

"We were hoping to find your Aunt Ruth," Adam said. "I'm glad you're here."

"She and Sam are at the Claremont Hotel in the Berkeley Hills," Tim said. "Come in and meet Artie and Teresa. Artie and his partner, Arturo, are the owners of this establishment and Teresa is my Aunt Ruth's upstairs neighbor on Collingwood Street just around the corner. She used to be my upstairs neighbor until I moved around the corner in the other direction and my Aunt Ruth moved into my old apartment."

"It sounds complicated," Alexandra said with a smile.

"Well, Adam knows where Ben and Jane and the kids live. They're my tenants and my downstairs neighbors. By the way, Adam, I saw you in the park with Sarah this morning, but I was too stoned to talk to you." Tim stopped and took a deep breath. He still felt a little stoned. "Man, I'm starting to talk like Patrick, now…"

Artie reached across the bar to shake hands with Adam and then Alex. Without looking in his direction, Artie said, "Sit down, Tim."

"And shut up!" Teresa added, before she shook hands with the couple. "Welcome to the Castro, kids. It's either the gayest little street in the universe or the murder capitol of the world. Take your pick."

"Murder?" Alex asked. "What's this all about, Adam?"

The three lesbians at the front corner of the bar got up and moved their drinks to a table, so Artie suggested that everyone sit down. "Can I get anyone a drink? We make great Bloody Marys, or how about a Ramos Fizz?"

"I'd love a cup of coffee," Alex said.

"I'll try one of your Bloody Marys," Adam said, pulling a fifty out of his wallet. "How about you, Tim? Teresa? May I buy you something?"

Teresa started to refuse until she glanced toward the front door at the same time Tim did. Someone appeared to be juggling a purse, the door, and several large shopping bags, all at the same time. It had to be Cousin Dianne. No self-respecting drag queen would go out on Castro Street looking this bad. She looked frazzled and angry with a lopsided scarf on her head and her slip was showing.

"Oh, God, look who's here," Tim said. "Now I really *need* a drink. I'd love a Bloody Mary. Thanks, Adam."

"You might as well make me one, too," Teresa said. "I won't face this woman sober if I don't have to. I ought to just go home and wait for Peter to call me when he's finished."

"Sit down, Teresa," Artie said.

"And *you* shut up. You're not leaving me alone with Cousin Dianne at a time like this." Tim spun around on his stool with his back to the door as if he didn't notice the commotion.

When Adam stood up to hold the door open for Dianne, Tim finally turned back around and said, "Well, if it isn't my delightful cousin Dianne! What a nice surprise to see you here. You remember Adam, don't you? He was at Sam's place down in Hillsborough at the same time we were. I'm sure you two were introduced."

"Maybe we were. They all look alike to me."

Artie gasped at Dianne's remark and Teresa lunged for her Bloody Mary. Adam, the perfect gentleman, acted as if he didn't hear it and tried to help with Dianne's shopping bags, but she only tightened her grip and ignored him. She wrestled them toward the bar and plopped down on a stool next to Teresa. "I thought my mother would be here. Where is she? I can't carry all this stuff up the hill by myself!"

"Is all of this shopping from downtown?" Tim asked. "Where's your rental car?"

"No, you dummy. Yesterday's shopping is back at Mother's apartment, except for what I already shipped back to Texas. These are some things I picked up here in the neighborhood today. The car is on Collingwood. I know better than to give up a good parking spot like that!"

"How was your trip to the spa?" Tim asked. "I heard they gave you the royal treatment."

"It was okay. I'm still sore from that masseuse. She was a huge Swedish woman who treated me like a slab of meat."

"It looks like you've been doing some serious shopping," Teresa said.

"Well, I picked up some gifts at that place across the street. Under One Roof, I think it's called, wedged in there between those *other* stores... disgusting!"

Tim said, "But you never know when a nice big dildo will come in handy, Dianne, especially when you get back to Texas."

She ignored him. "Yesterday I bought some cute outfits downtown, but the salesgirls in this city are so rude! They would never get away with that kind of attitude in Houston or Dallas."

"Whatever do you mean, Dianne?" Artie asked.

"They were entirely too *familiar*, if you ask me," Dianne grimaced. "What time is it, anyway? Is it too early for a glass of wine?"

"Not at all," Teresa said as she took a sip of her drink. "The sun's over the yardarm someplace!"

"Take the cost of her wine out of here." Adam pushed the change from his fifty toward the edge of the bar.

"I can buy my own glass of wine, thank you very much! I just have to find my purse among all these shopping bags." She pulled her scarf the rest of the way off her head and reached down to rummage through her belongings until she came up with her wallet.

"Your hair looks great, Dianne," Tim said. "Almost natural. It must have taken them hours to get all the shellac out of it and they lowered your head by at least three inches."

Dianne stuck her tongue out at Tim as she bent down to look for her purse. "I just hope it doesn't look too... too..."

Everyone's eyes were on Dianne as she crouched lower and lower. "I hope it doesn't look..." she started again, but her eyes rolled back in her head and she fainted dead away on the floor.

Tim and Teresa jumped off their barstools and knelt on either side of her. "Dianne, can you hear me?" Tim touched her forehead.

Teresa reached for Dianne's wrist to look for a pulse. At that moment, Peter Parker and Captain O'Sullivan came through the door from the kitchen. Tim and Teresa stepped back to give them room as O'Sullivan pulled the radio from his belt. "We need an ambulance right away. Arts bar and restaurant on Castro Street between 18th and 19th... Her pulse is weak, but she's breathing. Hurry!"

# Chapter 15

Fog swirled around the stranger on Collingwood Street. He pulled his collar up and admitted to himself that he might be in for a long wait. A mouthful of whiskey from his silver flask burned its way down his throat, warmed his stomach and spread heat through his lanky frame.

He'd stuck around the restaurant earlier, long enough to hear all he needed to hear and no one suspected him, he was sure. After the ambulance hauled off the snooty daughter, her faggot cousin got his aunt on the phone. From the faggot's end of the conversation, he gathered that she and the rich old boyfriend had spent one night at a ritzy hotel in the Oakland Hills. In the morning he surprised her with a drive up to Tahoe for a Chris Isaak concert. She gave up front row seats to fly back to the side of her ailing daughter.

He sure wouldn't, but then... he and the wife had never had kids.

He slipped the flask back inside his coat pocket. Then he reached across to the other side and felt for his gun. The weight of steel in his hand warmed him almost as much as the whiskey. Both the gun and the bullet would be easy to trace, but that didn't matter. It was a standard police-issue 40-caliber Beretta—reported missing months ago when an anti-war rally at the Civic Center got out of hand. He might even drop the gun right there when he was finished. Why make it harder for the cops? It wouldn't do them any good anyway. Gloves assured against fingerprints.

That busybody woman—Ruth Taylor—reminded him of his wife, always sticking her nose where it didn't belong. He coughed up a glob of phlegm and aimed it at the root of a tree. That was what he thought of his wife too. If it wasn't for her—always wanting something he couldn't afford—he wouldn't have to be mixed up in this business. There was no way to make that woman happy.

Ruth Taylor was the same type, but she'd found herself a millionaire boyfriend now. Sure, she still worked part-time at that queer joint on Castro Street, maybe to impress the old man, as if he cared. All she was doing was taking a job away from some poor homo who probably needed the hours worse than she did. Hell, he was doing everyone a favor by getting rid of that broad. Once the millionaire put a ring on her finger, she'd bleed him dry too. She was just like his wife.

Another swirl of fog enveloped him and the flask grew lighter with each swallow.

A couple of blocks away, Nick and Tim held hands across the table while they waited for their food. Their passionate reunion in Tim's bed, followed by a trip to Davies Hospital to wait for Aunt Ruth, had worked up their appetites. "The back booth at Orphan Andy's wasn't exactly the setting I had in mind for our first meal together in a while. I just couldn't think of where else we could go without even taking a shower first, but I was starving. I'm still kinda sticky. I hope you're not disappointed."

"Don't be silly, Snowman," Nick rubbed the flesh of his thumb across the backs of Tim's knuckles, one finger at a time. "We can eat at Fleur de Lys another time. It'll still be there tomorrow and besides, we can make out here if we want to." Nick leaned across the table and gave Tim a wet kiss on the nose.

"Didn't you get enough at my house?"

Nick grinned and shook his head as the waiter put their meals in front of them. "Let's see here… a bacon cheeseburger and fries for you, Tim… right? And you have the pancakes, eggs over easy, hash browns, bacon, sausage, and I'll be right back with some hot syrup… ready for more coffee?"

"Thanks," Tim said to the waiter and then asked Nick, "How can you eat breakfast at this hour of the night? You remind me of Jean-Yves."

"I can eat breakfast any time. And in answer to your question, no, I didn't get enough earlier. I can never get enough of you, Snowman."

"You smooth-talker." Tim shook the ketchup bottle and stared into Nick's eyes.

"And who's Jean Yves?"

"A Frenchman I used to know. He was a flight attendant who looked me up whenever he had a layover in San Francisco."

"A *lay* – over? I'll bet he did—"

"I wonder whatever became of him. It's been ages."

"You and your sordid past."

The gunman reached for the reassuring weight of the cold steel when a pair of headlights startled him. It was only a Jeep turning the corner by the Harvey Milk Civil Rights Academy. The driver was dressed in leather, probably looking for a parking place—some dude meeting friends for a drink in the Castro before they headed south of Market. Maybe he was going to his boyfriend's apartment to tie him up… to each his own. In a way, he had to hand it to the queers, though; they were free to do their thing, not stuck with a whiney woman who could never be satisfied.

He caught his shadowy reflection in a bay window and almost laughed out loud. He could pass for one of them tonight in his boots and jeans and leather coat. It was longer than a biker's jacket and the leather was brown instead of black, but no one would notice in this light. He was older than most of the guys who cruised Collingwood Park on foot. He didn't look out of place, though. He might be out here looking to score some fleeting anonymous sex... or drugs.

Drugs, hah! He never touched 'em! If these kids wanted to fry their brains, it was fine by him. He was happy to take their money. It was all business, as far as he was concerned—good business, raking in big bucks on his share alone and he didn't have to get his hands dirty. Well, there was that boy he'd been forced to dispose of, but at least he didn't have to deal with the chemistry lab.

Cutting up that boy was as easy as butchering a pig—shit happened when people got in the way, that's all. Let that be a lesson to the rest of them. Somebody had to be the enforcer. He was good at killing and he didn't know crap about manufacturing the stuff, but that's what his partners were for.

"The Enforcer," he said out loud. He liked the sound of it and that's what his job was. That's what he was good at, being *The Enforcer*. He got more respect for it than he ever did at his other job and a hell of a lot more respect than he ever got at home.

When they found the fingers and the eyeball it should have been enough to scare anyone. Hell, he hadn't even meant to lose the eyeball. It just got away from him and slipped down the drain, but they found it. They should have had enough sense to stay out of the way after that. But no, that busybody barmaid and the old lady in black had to stick their noses in.

The old lady was the one who called the police, but that's what you'd expect an old lady to do. She didn't live in the city and she didn't drive so he didn't worry so much about her getting in the way. He just had to teach that Taylor woman a lesson and a bullet through the head was a pretty good teacher. If need be, he'd take care of the old lady later. At her age, accidents happened all the time.

He'd thought about waiting to ambush her at the hospital tonight. She must still be there now at the daughter's bedside, even though it was past visiting hours. There were places he could have hidden in the bushes, but getting away afterward might have been a problem. And if he didn't kill her outright, she'd be right there at the emergency room where the doctors might save her. She'd be much too close to salvation for him to take that chance.

Now his partners would have to move the meth lab from Hartford Street and find a whole new spot for the operation. It was lucky they still had plenty of merchandise to sell in the meantime. He would hate for their regular customers to find a new source.

Tim worked a couple of French fries through a puddle of ketchup on his plate. "God, I hate hospitals... especially emergency rooms. Thanks for waiting with me until Aunt Ruth got back. I couldn't pretend to be as concerned about Dianne as I knew her mother would be."

"No problem, Snowman. I've gotten used to waiting around hospitals since I've known you."

"At least they took her to Davies—it's within walking distance—not that Dianne has made any friends in the Castro who would come to see her. It'll be convenient for Aunt Ruth, though. Did you get enough to eat? You've been shoveling it in like a field hand!"

"I guess I did work up an appetite. What do you think is wrong with your cousin, anyway? Has anyone talked to her husband in Texas?"

"Aunt Ruth tried to call him, but nobody seems to know where he is. Apparently they're taking 'separate vacations' this year. And the doctors won't know what's wrong until the tests come back. I'm just glad Sam is there with Aunt Ruth—almost as glad as I am that you're here with me."

"Me too, Snowman," Nick smiled and placed his big strong hand across the table for Tim to take hold of again. "Me too."

*The Enforcer* saw another set of lights turn the corner now. This time he felt lucky. It was a black limousine with a driver in uniform and the rest of the windows tinted so dark he couldn't see inside. He placed his finger on the trigger, still deep in his pocket and stepped behind the tree out of the headlights. The car angled into the driveway, but it was too long to fit all the way in.

He walked downhill to the next tree and stopped again as the driver set the parking brake and got out to open the passenger door.

Damn! She had the millionaire with her. What was the boyfriend's name? Sam, he thought it was. The millionaire reminded him of the retired army General Wesley Clark. Between the limo driver and the General, there was no way to get a clean shot at the broad. He stared down the sight of the gun as the three of them reached the gate, but she was shorter than both the men. She was already inside when the boyfriend took their bags from the chauffer on the doorstep and said a few words he couldn't hear. Then the driver got back in the car and pulled away and it looked like the millionaire was in there with her for the night.

Damn it all! It was a good thing he had a back-up plan. He returned the gun to his pocket and walked down the hill on Collingwood Street to Delano's 24-Hour Supermarket where he'd left his car. A pair of men held hands while they walked their faggoty little dog. There was nothing but homos out here tonight. Another queer wore skin-tight pants with holes all over them and a jacket open down the front to show off his bare chest—on a night like this!? This one stepped out of the shadows and right up close. "Gotta light?"

"I don't smoke."

"Too bad… you party?"

"Not with the likes of you!"

"Ass-hole!"

"Faggot!"

The queer tried to spit at him, but missed. It was well past time to get out of here before he caught something worse than a cold. The wife had told him to pick up a loaf of bread, a dozen eggs and half-gallon of milk so he stopped into Delano's. Aside from a boy stocking shelves and one lonely checker, the place looked deserted. He paid for the groceries with cash. At least now there'd be one less thing for her to bitch about when he got home.

# Chapter 16

Sunday morning was the first time in months that Tim and Nick could sleep late, cuddle up together and make out without any of Tim's bandages or casts in the way. This weekend felt almost as hot as their first time together... or better. The sublime comfort of familiarity and trust made up for the thrill of newness. And Nick was right about Fleur de Lys. It was still there the next day and for countless Sundays afterward. They never went to eat there in order to find out, but it would have made the news if it had burned down.

The two of them had so much fun having sex together that Tim felt foolish for pushing Nick away lately. The soreness from Tim's accident had completely left him, his paranoia melted away and he had never felt so loved.

Nick had to go back up north on Sunday evening, so Tim woke up alone on Monday morning. Now he felt a little sore and achy, but that might have been the result of so much strenuous exercise in bed. He reached for Nick, but only found his pillow, so he buried his face in Nick's scent and tried to get back to sleep. He had nothing on his schedule for today except some long-neglected housecleaning chores. He might throw a load of wash into the machine, but not this pillowcase... not yet.

The doorbell rang as Tim poured water into the coffee maker, so he pulled on a robe on his way to the front of the house. "Aunt Ruth!" Tim yelled down from the window. "What's going on?"

"If you let me in, I'll tell you. I hope I didn't wake you boys, but I sure could use a cup of coffee."

Tim buzzed her in and started opening windows. He no longer smelled Nick's hair, but the place reeked of sex—sweat, pot, lube and poppers. The living room smelled more like a locker room and the day was already getting warm, by San Francisco standards. Tim looked around and spotted his crumpled blue jeans in front of the fireplace. His jockey shorts were on the floor beside the arm of the couch, where Nick had pulled them off him last night. "Come on in the kitchen with me, Aunt Ruth. I just put the coffee on."

"How about getting a big hug from my favorite nephew first? Where's Nick?"

"He drove back to Monte Rio late last night. He had to be at the nursery first thing this morning to accept a delivery. Some of the new greenhouses are far enough along to start stocking them with seedlings."

"Did you two have a good time together, dear?"

"The best ever," Tim answered with an ear-to-ear grin.

"It shows on your face this morning."

Tim wiped the corners of his mouth, even though that wasn't what she'd meant. "I tried your cell phone and then I called the Claremont and they said you'd already checked out, but I couldn't reach you in Tahoe, either."

"We had a lovely time until we had to rush back, of course."

"Oh, right. I keep erasing Dianne from my memories. Nick and I got out of there as soon as you showed up the other night. We were starved. And then we spent most of yesterday… So, how is my dear cousin?"

"She's stable, but still sedated." Ruth blew on her coffee.

"Can we keep her that way?"

Aunt Ruth frowned. "I'm on my way over to the hospital now and I was hoping you'd come with me. Sam went back to Hillsborough to take care of business this morning, too. Dianne's doctors said they might have some more of the test results back today. I know she's not your favorite person, nor does she deserve to be. She's been incredibly rude to you and—"

"I'll be glad to go along for your sake, if not hers. It'll do me good to get out of the house, anyway. Aside from a trip to the emergency room and a late-night dinner at Orphan Andy's, I've have been holed up here since Saturday night and here it is Monday morning. Should we take the T-Bird?"

No, let's walk. It's only a few blocks."

They found Dianne sitting up in bed. She looked pale, but alert. Ruth gave her a peck on the cheek. "What beautiful flowers. Who are they from?"

"I don't know and I don't care!"

Tim read the card and let out a laugh.

"What's so damned funny?" Dianne snatched the card from Tim. Her lips moved as she read the inscription. "This says they're from you, Tim. Did you send me flowers?"

"No, that's what's so funny. Nick must have sent them and signed my name as a joke. So, did the doctors say you're at death's door or will you live to torture your mother and me another day?"

"The doctors just left." Dianne turned toward Ruth. "You'd better sit down, Mother. Move those things off that chair and pull it closer to me so I don't have to shout."

"What is it, dear?" Ruth sat and tried to take Dianne's hand, but it was snatched away. "What did the doctors say?"

"It's my kidneys. I knew they were failing, but I thought I had more time. I need to start dialysis soon if I can't find a transplant. The doctors want to talk to you about being a donor. That's the only reason I came to California in the first place."

Ruth stared across the bed at Tim and turned as white as the hospital sheets.

"Aunt Ruth, are you alright?"

Ruth blinked a couple of times and the color slowly returned to her face. She stared out the window and finally spoke without looking at either Tim or Dianne. "There's something you need to know, Dianne. I would have told you a long time ago, but I promised not to... not unless it came to something like this."

"What is it, Mother?"

"Do you remember my old college friend, Cindy? She and Jack lived in St. Louis Park during most of the years while you were growing up in Edina."

"Sure, I remember," Dianne said. "We kids called it St. Jewish Park. I never understood why you wanted to be friends with a person like that. What has this got to do with *me*, Mother?"

"I'm getting to that. First, I just wanted to make sure you remembered her."

"Yeah, I remember when you had her baby-sit me in that big old house sometimes, but I always thought she was weird. What about her?"

"Cindy and I met at Stanford, where we grew into the best of friends. We even roomed together during our senior year." Ruth paused and stared out the window again for a minute. "We also both got pregnant at the same time..."

"So?"

Tim could see where this confession might lead and he could hardly believe what he was hearing, but Dianne was oblivious to anything that wasn't directly and obviously related to her. "Well, neither of us was married, of course, so Cindy and I considered ourselves lucky to have each other's support during that time. Dan and I decided to get married as soon as I started to show, but Cindy—"

"Don't tell me," Dianne interrupted. "She got herself knocked up by some guy who wouldn't do the right thing by her. How typical of a woman like that."

"Dianne, let me finish!" Ruth glared at her. "Cindy and Jonathan were crazy about each other. Jonathan Goldstein. I've hardly thought of him in all these years. Cindy's family heartily approved of him, a good Jewish boy, going places. When I say 'approved' I meant they approved of them *dating*. Cindy's parents lived in Boston and Jonathan came from upstate New York. No one but Cindy and I had an inkling that a grandchild was on the way. That would have been a different matter, especially back then."

Tim hadn't been aware of holding his breath until he let it out. "Thank goodness times have changed and people are more enlightened nowadays. I don't know whether or not that's true in Texas, but—"

"Don't interrupt," Dianne snapped at Tim.

Ruth stood up and walked over to the window before she continued. "Dan and I got married and Cindy knew Jonathan would have married her, if he'd known about the baby, but his number came up in the lottery and the next thing we knew he was on his way to Viet Nam."

"What number?" Dianne asked. "What lottery? What does this have to do with me?"

"You never were much of a history buff, were you, Dianne?" Tim asked. "Even I knew about the lottery!"

"Shut up!"

Ruth turned back from the window. "They drew numbers—birthdates—to see who had to go into the Army first. Jonathan had a student deferment, but he'd let it lapse to go back East for a family crisis. I forget what it was, but he no sooner got back to California when he was drafted and shipped off to basic training. Then he was killed in Viet Nam on his first week over there. Cindy never even told him she was having his baby."

"How awful," Tim said.

"Cindy and I went into labor on the same day. We figured the babies must have been conceived on a weekend camping trip the four of us took together." Ruth smiled for a moment, remembering a pleasant respite in the midst of a nightmare.

Then her face lost its color and she went on, "We went to the hospital and Cindy's labor was smooth as could be. I got sick. I was burning up with fever and chills. The doctors thought they might lose me and my baby. They told me later I could never get pregnant again or it might kill me."

Dianne let out a yawn and interrupted, "So… what on earth does this old story about you have to do with my kidneys?"

"My baby was a boy, Dianne! He was stillborn. To make a long story short, we decided that I would adopt you before we even left the hospital. Cindy's parents back East never had to find out she was pregnant and I still had a baby to love and raise as my own, just as I'd planned. I promised Cindy she could see you all she wanted, but we would never tell anyone about it… unless something like this happened."

"How could you pull off a trick like that?" Dianne asked the question that was on Tim's mind too.

"It was a small private hospital and both my parents were still alive at the time. My father—you were too little to remember him—but he was a very powerful man and the whole plan just made perfect sense. Cindy would be able to see you all she wanted and watch you grow up, but she could also finish her education without the stigma of being an unwed mother. In those days things were a little different, you know?"

"You mean my own mother didn't want me?" Dianne asked.

"That's not what I said, Dianne! Of course we *all* wanted you. I raised you as my own daughter. Cindy moved to Minnesota so that she could be nearby. Dan adored you. You're still his little girl."

"I can't believe you could get away with something like that."

"Don't worry. The adoption was all handled legally. It took a while for all the paperwork to be ironed out, but nobody else ever needed to know the whole truth. Not until now."

"Oh my God!" Dianne screamed. "I just thought of something else. If she was my real mother, that means I'm a Jew! I can't believe it. I'd rather be Chinese!"

Tim giggled and said, "Don't forget the 'B' word!"

"I've been called a bitch before and it doesn't bother me, you faggot!"

"Bitch works too, but the 'B' I was talking about was 'bastard,' you bigot! Hey, there's another 'B' word that fits you."

Dianne reached for the call button to summon the nurse. "Get him out of here! I can't take any more of this!"

Tim stood up. "Don't stress yourself. I'm leaving anyway. I'll wait outside, Aunt Ruth. Good luck with the bigot... bastard... bitch... bible-thumping bimbo... boor... brat..." His words trailed behind him.

"What about me?" Dianne was hysterical now. "What about my kidneys? You're not even my real mother! You're no use to me now."

"Your birth mother may be able to help you, though. Cindy and Jack moved to Boston a few years ago, after their youngest, the twins, graduated high school. You have eight healthy half-brothers and sisters. There's a good chance you might find a donor among them, I imagine."

"Is everything alright in here?" Dianne and Ruth looked toward the doorway as the nurse, a young black man, walked in. "It sounded like someone was in trouble."

"I'm afraid that Dianne has just received some very unsettling news."

"I can't believe you lied to me all these years!"

"I'm sure this must come as a shock to you, Dianne, but I want you to know that all of us did what we thought was best for everyone involved, especially you, at the time..."

The nurse said, "It's time for your medication, anyway. This should help you sleep."

"Why can't everybody just leave me alone?"

"Try to get some rest, Dianne, and we'll talk more later." Ruth started toward the door but signaled to the nurse that she would wait for him in the hallway. Ruth paced until he came out of the room a few minutes later. "Is she alright?"

"She's sleeping now. Her doctor ordered intravenous sedatives as needed after the last time she became disruptive. She should sleep for a while now."

"My cell phone number is on her chart as her emergency contact. Would you please call me if she needs me or if there's any change at all?"

"Are you her mother?"

"Close enough..." Ruth rode the elevator down and walked outside the hospital doors where Tim stood in the sunshine with a big smile on his face, waiting to give her a big hug and walk her home.

# Chapter 17

Tim and Ruth walked down Castro Street from Davies hospital. "I've got to hand it to you, Aunt Ruth. You sure know how to keep a secret. I can't believe you've kept all that inside you for so many years."

Ruth nodded, more to herself than to her nephew. "I've gotten so used to the way things were that I rarely think about how they got that way. You know me. I try to live in the present. And when you stick with a story long enough it starts to feel like the truth. I'm so sorry that it had to come out like this."

"I'm sorry I called her a bastard... but not the other things.

Ruth patted him on the arm. "It's understandable. After you've endured her insults for so many years."

"You know, as hard as I try..." Tim started.

"What is it, dear?"

"I'm sorry, but as hard as I try to muster up some sympathy for my 'cousin' Dianne and her medical problems; what I honestly feel is relief."

"Relief?"

"She isn't related to me by even one single drop of blood."

"Oh, Tim—"

"Or to you either." Tim stopped and hugged her. "To be honest, I was growing a bit jealous ever since she came to the city. I didn't want to lose being your favorite."

"Honey, I raised Dianne as best I could and I've called her my own for so many years there's no erasing that. We'll always have some history, but the real connection I have is with you."

"Maybe her birth mother will part with a kidney… or one of her kids," Tim said, "if Dianne will accept a kidney from a Jewish person."

Someone called their names from the window of a Yellow Cab. "Where are you two going?" The taxi pulled up beside them and Adam got out.

"Hey, Adam. I'm walking my Aunt Ruth back home from the hospital. What are you up to?"

"I'm on my way to the hospital to pay Dianne a visit. Sam wanted to come, but he's tied up with work. He asked me to stop by in his place, since I'm in San Francisco. He hoped I could catch you, Ruth. He sends his love."

"Where's Alexandra?" Tim asked. He still didn't know whether Sam had told Ruth about Adam, but there had been enough confessions for one day.

"When I left the hotel she was just getting out of bed. We're staying at the Ritz Carlton. She wants to do some shopping before we fly back to L.A. tonight. How is Dianne?"

"She should be resting comfortably by now," Ruth said. "How nice of you to come by, but there's no sense in trying to see her right now. The nurse just gave her something to help her sleep."

"Well, I promised Alex I'd meet her for lunch if I got back in time. Oh good, here's another cab," Adam waved to a Luxor driver who made a u-turn. "We'll see you both soon, I hope."

"Give our regards to Alex, okay?" Tim waved.

"Have a nice lunch!" Ruth shouted to Adam as he climbed into the taxi. "What a charming young man, don't you think so, Tim?"

"Yes, very…"

"How nice of him to come and see about Dianne," Ruth said. "I mean, she hasn't been very nice to him, either... of course, it's not like she was *family* to *him*, whether I was her birth mother or not...and she can be such a nasty racist, too."

Tim thought that was an odd thing to say about family. Now he was really curious as to how much Sam had told her. When Ruth and Sam got married, Adam would become her stepson, definitely "family," as far as Ruth was concerned, as well as Tim's "step-cousin?" He wasn't sure what to call that. Tim liked the idea of being related to Adam a lot more than being related to Dianne.

They crossed Market Street and continued south toward Cliff's Variety. Ruth dropped a dollar in the case of an accordion player who entertained the pigeons in the plaza outside Twin Peaks bar. The sun dissipated the patchy clouds overhead; a beautiful day was in store. Tim noticed Patrick at the bulletin board beside the entrance to the Castro Theatre parking lot. He turned his head to the right, as if he recognized a friend across the street, but Patrick saw them, too. "Hiya, Tim! Hey, Tim's Aunt Ruth! Remember me?"

"Hello Patrick," Ruth said with a smile. "Of course I remember you. You're looking well."

"Are you posting flyers for your E.T. project?" Tim asked Patrick and started to explain to Ruth, "He's involved with helping people stay off crystal—"

"No, these are pictures of my missing friend Darryl. Remember when I saw you in the park I told you he went to Santa Barbara, but when I didn't hear from him after he should have gotten back, I called down there and they told me he never showed up for his grandmother's funeral. His family acted kind of like they didn't expect him, anyway. I guess they got used to him being a flake. Still, I know he's not like that anymore. He's responsible, now. We both have a new way of life now that we're clean and sober."

Ruth peered at one of the flyers. "I'm afraid I've never seen your friend. Is this a recent picture?"

"About a month ago," Patrick said. "It was the best I could find. He shaved his head since then. There in the picture it's just really short with sort of a Mohawk. His moustache is usually longer than that, and you almost never see him without a tiny gold hoop earring through his right nostril, but for some reason he wasn't wearing it when that picture was taken. Anybody who saw this would recognize him, though. He has the most beautiful green eyes! I just went by Arts but they weren't open yet. Tim, could you take a couple of these flyers and put them up there for me later?"

"I'll be glad to do it, " Ruth said. "I was planning to stop in there later and have a look at the schedule anyway. Now that Artie's back is better I'm not sure whether he still needs me at all anymore. He's probably forgotten all about me."

"I'm sure he wouldn't do that," Patrick said. "Everybody loves to come in when you're working. It's like buying drinks from your Mom if your Mom was cool."

"Thank you. I'm sure you mean that as a compliment."

"You bet. You know… the cops gave me all kinds of grief when I tried to file a missing person's report, since Darryl was from L.A. and a recovering addict and all, but they finally took down the information when I found a gay cop to talk to. I don't think they'll give his case much priority, though. One less druggie—clean or not—is good news for the police department. That's why I'm putting up these flyers.

"How did it go the other night in Collingwood Park? Wasn't it Saturday night when you were handing out those E.T. flyers?"

"It was really cold out, so it was pretty slow. The fog was so thick there was hardly anybody on the streets after the bars closed. The homeless people we saw weren't tweakers, for the most part. Their drug of choice is usually alcohol. If they want to talk, we will. I mean, we can direct them to a shelter or something, but we're mostly looking for speed freaks."

"That was the night you raced back from Tahoe to the hospital," Tim said to Ruth.

"Oh, that was a cold one," Ruth agreed. "You had Nick to keep you warm."

Patrick said, "Yeah, there were a few people walking their dogs and a handful of die-hards out cruising, but hardly any tweakers. With Delano's open all night and Walgreens too, there are usually people out at all hours, but that fog got so thick you could hardly see across the street."

"That reminds me—" Tim started to say.

But Patrick wasn't finished talking and there was no stopping him. "I'd rather be south of Market on nights like that, where there's some action. They don't like us hanging out in the doorway of Delano's, but sometimes that's the only place to keep warm. Well, I'd better get going. Darryl could be anywhere. I just hope he's not using again. I still have to hit the Tenderloin and Polk Street with these flyers, but thanks for putting one up at Arts for me, Ruth. If you see Darryl, please call me or else call that number and tell him I'm looking for him, okay? We all are. Bye."

Patrick continued north while Ruth and Tim walked on to the corner where they crossed 18th Street. "I need to stop at Walgreens and see if my prescription is ready. You don't need to wait for me unless you want to."

"I'll run along home, then. I'm sure I'll have tons of mail to sort through—mostly bills—and plants to water. I haven't checked my e-mail all weekend. Thanks for walking me to the hospital, sweetheart."

"No problem," Tim said. One of the same flyers Patrick was handing out had been taped up inside the window of Walgreens. "I hope Patrick finds his friend Darryl."

"Me, too," Ruth said. She never imagined for a minute that she would be the one to find him first.

# Chapter 18

"Yoo-hoo! Ruthie... anybody home?" Teresa found her neighbor's door standing wide open so she stuck her head inside and hollered down the hallway.

"Come on in. I'm in the kitchen."

"Did you know that your door was wide op... oh... sorry... I didn't know you were on the phone."

"It's okay... I've been on hold for hours! Come in and sit down. Do you want some coffee? I'll put on a fresh pot. I've been trying to call my ex in Minneapolis and I'm not having much luck getting through at his office. You'd think we were still married."

"No thanks, hon. I've had it up to here with coffee, already. I just wondered why your door was wide open. Where's the kitty cat?"

"I don't know. That's why I left the door open. I'm hoping he'll come back. I just got home a little while ago and the minute I walked inside he took off between my legs like a bolt of lightening. Then he squeezed through the gate and ran off down the hill. Poor Bartholomew! He's been so miserable lately."

"Well, he was as sweet as could be when he stayed up at my place those couple of nights you and Sam were away. I wonder what's gotten into him."

"I suppose he's mad at me for leaving him alone. You know how cats are."

"Yes indeed, they have major abandonment issues... or is that dogs? We had a dog once when I was a little girl in Seattle that..."

Ruth held up the palm of her hand to interrupt Teresa and then she spoke into the telephone again, "Yes, I'm still here. Yes, I can continue holding. Yes, I'm... No, I didn't... Excuse me? No, I am trying to reach Dan Taylor. This is his ex-wife, Ruth. Someone told me he was in a meeting, but that it was about to wrap up and that I should stay on the... Yes, I'll hold."

Ruth poured herself a cup of cold coffee and put it in the microwave. "I won't make a fresh pot if you're not having any. I'll just reheat some of this; it can't be that bad. By the way, thanks for taking care of Bart on short notice."

"Any time," Teresa reassured her. "I just wonder where he's gone off to now."

"He spent the whole night right inside the back door and this morning he wouldn't eat a thing. I carried him with me to the living room, but as soon as I sat down he jumped out of my arms and ran back to the kitchen. Dianne's things are still in the front so I suppose he can smell her scent. I've never known a cat to dislike anyone so much. It makes me wonder what kind of awful things she's been doing to him when I'm not around."

"My mother always says cats are even better judges of character than dogs. I was kind of glad to have Bartholomew at my house while Peter was there. When I watched Peter pick him up real gentle-like and rub his belly it gave me a good feeling about the man. And Bart just purred and stretched out on his lap like an old hooker..."

"Oh my," Ruth laughed.

"Well, you know it just made me want to do the same thing!"

Ruth laughed. "You and Peter seem to be hitting it off well."

"Knock on wood," Teresa tapped the table leg with her right knuckle. "So far so good. I've never dated a cop before. On the one hand I worry about him being in danger all the time when he's at work, but on the other hand, that uniform is kind of sexy."

"Just a second," Ruth said, and then spoke into the phone again. "Yes, I'm right here waiting. Where else would I be? Is Dan still in his meeting or not?"

Ruth's doorbell rang and she gave Teresa a wide-eyed look of exasperation, mouthing, "Now, what?"

Teresa said, "Sit tight, honey. I'll go see who it is. It's probably a solicitor. I'll get rid of them. Or maybe someone's returning Bartholomew."

"Now they've got me on hold again, but who knows how long it will be this time? I ask you, is this any way to run a business? What if I were an important client or something?"

Teresa was already down the hallway by now and didn't hear Ruth's complaints. "Hello!" She called out as she walked down the steps to the gate, but there was no response. She turned the knob, stepped out onto the sidewalk and held the gate open with one hand but she couldn't see anyone walking away in either direction. As Teresa stepped back inside she spotted a small white box, narrow enough to fit between the bars Bartholomew had squeezed through to get out.

She carried the box back to Ruth's kitchen and said, "We should talk to Arturo and Artie about putting up some kind of a screen on that gate. If the cat can get out, the raccoons must be able to get in… or worse things… like rats."

Ruth shouted into the phone, "I have already *been* on hold for nearly half an hour! First you said Dan was in a meeting and told me to wait on the line. Now, you can't find him? Yes, I'll hold. What choice do I have at this point?"

Teresa picked up one of the flyers Ruth had left on the side table and looked at the picture of Patrick's missing friend Darryl. "Where did these come from?"

"You remember Patrick, don't you? He was that clean-cut blond boy who worked as a waiter at Arts with Tim."

"The one who went away to rehab? This doesn't look a bit like him, I'm afraid."

"No, that's a picture of Patrick's friend Darryl. They met at the Betty Ford clinic, I take it, and now Darryl has turned up missing. I promised Patrick I'd post a couple of those at Arts when I go to work. Who was at the door? What have you got there?"

"Nobody," Teresa said. "Somebody left this box, though. I thought it was from a florist, but they must have jumped into a car and split as soon as they rang your bell. Why would a florist do that, I wonder? It looks like someone printed your name in crayon across the top. A florist would have attached a nice card, wouldn't they?"

"That is my name, isn't it? I can barely read that scrawl," Ruth said and then shouted into the telephone, "What do you mean, he's out of town? How could he be in a meeting one minute and out of town the next? Do you have a helicopter on your roof nowadays? No. No, I don't. Yes, I've been waiting for over half an hour. You could at least take a message for him. Tell him to call his ex-wife. He has the number. No, my name is Ruth. It's Ruth Taylor! How many ex-wives does he have by now? I'm the one in San Francisco! Thank you very much. You have a nice day too, dear."

Ruth dropped the phone into its cradle. "Unbelievable! I have never seen such incompetence. What a way to do business! Wait until I get a hold of Dan. I'll give him a piece of my mind! I thought it was only right that I tell him about Dianne, but you'd think I was a bill-collector, the way they're treating me."

"Now, Ruth... there's a reason they're exes and not currents, right?"

"You're absolutely right. There's no sense letting him make me so angry. He did enough of that while we were married. He'll call me when he calls me and then maybe he'll be the one to have to wait around. Now, what have we here? You think someone sent me flowers, do you?"

"I thought at first it might be a corsage, but look how they stuck the lid on willy-nilly with Scotch tape all over the place. No gay florist would let the tape show like that."

"No, I guess not."

"Neither would any florist with any taste, gay or straight."

"Well, let's open it and see." Ruth reached for the box and started pulling at the tape, but soon gave up and fetched a pair of scissors from a kitchen drawer. She slid one blade around the edge of the box, cut the tape and removed the lid, but it looked to be full of crumpled newspaper.

"Honey, I don't know what this is, but I don't think it's any kind of gift."

"Well, it's not my birthday," Ruth said. "It's not any special day at all and if Sam were sending me something, there'd be a card, wouldn't there? Who else would send me something? I just don't know."

Teresa lifted the top layer of crumpled newspaper and spread out one corner to see the date. "It's this morning's Chronicle and look! Those look like Polaroids! Do they still even make film for Polaroid cameras? They're all blurry. I wonder what they're supposed to be."

"I don't know. Let me see them under the light." Ruth reached for them. "This top one looks like a picture of big green box."

"It's a refrigerator." Teresa said. "Lenny and I had one just like that in our first apartment when we got married. The landlord said he'd bought it at the old Sears store on Masonic and Geary and it still worked like new. It was a Kenmore side-by-side refrigerator freezer in avocado green. That fridge lasted a lot longer than our marriage, that's for sure."

Ruth had gone on to the second picture, which showed the freezer door standing open with a sunken-eyed face peering out from one of the otherwise empty shelves. "Look at this one. Is that a Halloween mask?" she asked Teresa. It appeared to be male and Caucasian, but it was otherwise unrecognizable. It had a frost-covered moustache and the head was misshapen, like a plastic doll partially melted from having been left in the sun, even though it was in a refrigerator.

"Oh God!" Teresa said, "That's no mask, Ruth. I think it's a real human head. Let's see that picture a little closer. That's gross. What's the other one?"

"The third one looks like the same picture. No, it isn't quite the same. The nose is missing. Oh, what kind of a sick joke is this?"

Teresa picked up the box and dumped the rest of the contents out onto Ruth's kitchen table. There was more crumpled newspaper, a zip-lock quart-size freezer bag, and a note that fluttered to the floor. Teresa let out a scream when the clear plastic bag hit the table. It held an eyeball and a nose with a tiny gold ring through the right nostril. Both were frozen, but thawing fast.

"Oh, my God. Patrick said Darryl wore a tiny gold hoop in his nose. I think these belonged to his missing friend."

Ruth jumped back from the table and cringed. She had begun to pick up the corner of the bag with her fingertips, but now she dropped it back down among the crumpled newspapers. She reached for the telephone and one of the flyers at the same time. "Let me see that picture again. No, I mean the second one. See it there? It's so frosty that it's hard to make out, but I think that's the same gold ring that's on the nose in this bag. Oh dear, I don't know who to call first. I must have Captain O'Sullivan's number around here somewhere. Maybe I left his card in my purse."

"Peter's number is right beside my bed. Don't you move a muscle, Ruthie. I'll run upstairs and get it and I'll be back in a jiffy."

Ruth had almost forgotten about the note that fell out of the box. She picked it up from the floor and read the scrawl under the bright kitchen light.

*Keep yore eyes 2 yoresef & yore own fat noz out of other peepls biznis if you no wats gud 4 you or yule B next, Bich!*

# Chapter 19

After Tim said good-bye to his Aunt Ruth he sat down on the bench outside Buffalo Whole Foods and punched in the number at the nursery. Jenny answered the phone. "Gosh, Tim, I know Nick would want to talk to you, but he's in an important meeting with a rich client who just bought a winery. I could tell him it's an emergency. You just say the word and I will. I mean, when he has a client in the 'inner sanctum' we're not supposed to disturb him, but..."

"That's okay, Jen..." Tim was dying to tell Nick the good news about having one less whack-job clinging to the family tree. Now he had to stifle a pang of paranoia that Nick wasn't available to him at a moment's notice.

"You should see his new office, Tim. It's really nice, now that the hardwood floors are finished and all the new furniture is moved in."

"I'm sure I'll see it soon. Just tell him I called, okay?"

"Wait a minute, Tim. We have some other rules around here I almost forgot. Nick said that whenever Tim calls, that's a priority, too."

Tim smiled at this bit of news.

"I'm just not sure which rule has priority, so if you said it was an emergency, I could interrupt his meeting. Either way, I'm gonna be in trouble."

"God, you make Nick sound like an ogre," Tim tried to laugh. "I'm glad I don't have to work for him and see his dark side."

"Oh, *no*! Now I'll be in trouble for saying that. Don't you dare make it sound like I said that. He's the best boss I've ever had. You tell him that. And furthermore, he's been in a terrific mood ever since he got back from seeing you this weekend."

Tim's paranoia vanished as quickly as it had surfaced. "I've got an idea. When Nick finishes his meeting, call me, but hang up after the first ring. I'll wait a minute and then I'll call him back. You and I never had this conversation and nobody gets in any trouble, okay?"

"You're the best! Thanks, Tim. Don't wait too long to call, though. If he signs a new account with this winery, he might want to knock off early and celebrate. Maybe he'll take me shopping for new gardening gloves at the K-Mart in Santa Rosa."

"What a thrill!"

"That's the story of my life, just one big thrill after another," Jenny laughed. "Later. "

"Thanks, Jen."

Tim snapped his cell phone shut and heard someone call his name. He looked around and saw Arturo waving from his car window across the street. He was pulling into a space a few yards uphill from the restaurant.

"Hi, Arturo," Tim yelled back, but was drowned out by the screeching siren of a passing ambulance. He crossed Castro Street and reached the car as Arturo popped open the trunk containing all the supplies from a major shopping trip at Costco.

"Your timing couldn't be better, Tim. You and Nick both seem to show up right when you're needed. How do you boys do it?"

"I think you're just lucky. But the last time Nick helped you out was when you guys found the body parts in the sewage. I hope you don't have any grisly surprises in store for me today."

"We are fresh out of eyeballs and severed limbs, I assure you. If you'll just carry the paper things inside, that will be a big help. They're the lightest ones. There's a case of envelopes, a case of paper towels, and—"

"I got it, Arturo. I got it." Arturo went ahead of Tim in order to turn off the alarm system and between the two of them they unloaded the car in three trips.

"I'd at least offer you a drink in return for helping me out, but you know Artie's the bartender in the family. How about a cold beer? I think I know how to open one of those without any trouble."

"That's alright," Tim said. "I'm okay. I just walked Aunt Ruth back to Collingwood from the hospital and I'm on my way home. I've got chores to do and I'm expecting a call from Nick."

"How is your cousin? Did she get her test results back yet? What's the verdict over there at the hospital?"

"Yeah, well..." Tim started to say, but he didn't want to explain everything to Arturo just now. He wanted to tell Nick the news, first. "It's kind of a long story. I'm sure Aunt Ruth will fill you in when she knows more. I've gotta get going."

"Thanks again for helping me out, Tim."

"Sure, no problem... do you need help putting things away?"

"Nah, that's okay... but one more thing before you go..."

"Yeah?"

"Artie and I were wondering if you're planning to come back to work soon. Business has been good lately. Lots of tourists in town these days and both Jake and James are overdue for some vacation time. It looks like we'll have to hire another waiter, but we wanted you to have first dibs."

"Thanks, Arturo. I really appreciate it and I'd like to say I could start tomorrow, but I'm not quite there, yet. A couple more weeks, maybe?"

"Two weeks... can we hold you to that?"

"Hey, what about Patrick? You know he's back in town, right? He says he's been clean for six months, now. He's involved with some new anti-meth crusade, but it's not like he's making any money at it."

"What do you think?" Arturo asked. "You've seen him. We haven't. Do you think he's really gotten himself straightened out?"

"I sure hope so. He told me you and Artie paid for him to go to Betty Ford. That was really good of you guys."

"Both times," Arturo turned and stared out the window toward the delivery truck unloading fifty-pound bags of potting soil in front of the plant store across the street. "We thought it was the right thing to do, that's all. He was a good kid before he got mixed up with that stuff. You know... after Jorge and Jason were killed, Artie and I got to thinking. You boys and our tenants—especially your Aunt Ruth—are like our little family. We were afraid if we didn't get Patrick straightened out, we might lose another one of our kids and we just couldn't take a chance on that."

"Then why not give him a chance to cover for one of those vacations you mentioned. You could see how he does."

"I'll talk it over with Artie. If you think Patrick is ready and you might be ready too in a couple of weeks, we could probably put you both on the schedule, at least part time. Then we wouldn't need to hire anyone." Arturo lifted one of the heavy boxes from the floor and set it on top of the bar.

"I'm sure I'll be ready to come back to work soon, but you might want to see how I do, too. I might be pretty rusty after so much time off."

Arturo smiled and shook his head. "I'm sure you'll do fine. I ought to just let Artie worry about handling the staff. He's had a lot more experience with people than me. I'm better off staying in the background. That reminds me, I need to put some of these cold things in the walk-in right away. I'll lock you out first. Thanks again for your help."

"Bye, Arturo."

Tim walked back up the hill to 19th Street and then left to Noe. As he reached in his pocket for his front door keys he felt his cell phone vibrate once and stop. Jenny. He was glad that Adam had showed him how to turn off the opening bars of *The 1812 Overture* and set the phone to vibrate. He'd told Jenny to let the phone ring once, but the vibrator had gone off twice already. Who could this be? Hardly anyone had the number.

A month or so ago he practically had to crawl up these stairs in torturous pain, but now he took them two at a time. Tim threw himself across his bed and flipped open the cell phone at the same time he kicked off his sneakers.

"Hey, Tim, is that you?" Jenny asked. "Are you home yet?"

"Yo, Jen! I just walked in the door."

"Perfect timing. The client just drove off and Nick came out of the office with a huge grin on his face."

"Great! Where is he? You were supposed to let it ring once and hang up. Can't he hear you? Are you going to let me talk to him this time?"

"He went to the bathroom. You can't hear anything in there with the fan running. Hold on a sec. Here he comes, now... Nick! It's Tim on line one!"

"Thanks a lot, Jen."

"I'll get it in my office." That was all Tim could hear in the background, followed by a couple of clicks and finally, "Hey, Snowman! What's up?"

"Nick, I've got the most amazing news about Dianne. I've been dying to tell someone."

"I've got good news, too," Nick said, "but you go first. What did the doctors say? Did she get the test results back?"

"Oh, that..." Tim paused. "That part isn't so good. She needs a kidney transplant eventually and she'll have to start dialysis soon."

"Too bad. I know she's a pain in the ass, but I wouldn't wish that on anyone. I had an uncle in New Orleans who went through that. What's the good news?"

"Well, it turns out that *Cousin Dianne* isn't really my cousin after all!"

"Your Aunt Ruth's daughter isn't really your cousin? How is that possible?"

"Aunt Ruth and Uncle Dan weren't her real parents. They switched the babies in the hospital right after Dianne was born."

"Gee, what a bummer! Are they gonna sue the hospital or is it too late for that?"

"No, it's not like that at all. Ruth's baby, my real cousin, was a boy. He was stillborn the same day that Dianne popped out. Her mother was Aunt Ruth's best friend, but she wasn't married and the father was killed in Viet Nam before he even knew she was pregnant."

"How could they get away with something like that?"

"I don't know. Who cares? Aunt Ruth said it was all done legally, but then no one ever talked about it again. All I know is I'm thrilled not to be related to that nasty woman."

"Wow! What does Dianne have to say about all this?"

"Get this." Tim said. "She's not as upset about being born to some woman who didn't happen to be married at the time… What did they call it back then?

"Politely?" Nick asked. "Out of wedlock. Impolitely… a bastard."

"Right, I already called her every B-word I could think of… bitch, bimbo, bigot… but 'out of wedlock'… it sounds kinda funny nowadays."

"Yeah, it does when you say it out loud."

"Wedlock." Tim laughed. "It sounds like some kind of bondage device or some kinky position or maybe a wrestling hold."

"Are you trying to get me excited, Snowman?"

"Hah. Not over the phone. You'll have to wait 'til I see you in person. But hey, can't you just hear someone complaining, 'we ordered our new wedlock from Fort Troff in Atlanta and then we found out we could have gotten one cheaper at Mr. S right here in San Francisco and not had to pay all those shipping costs."

Nick laughed and Tim went on, "Get this. Dianne is also Jewish!"

"Is that a problem for her, too?"

"Yes! She's one of those born-agains, you know. She freaked! She's so hateful she started screaming how she'd rather be Chinese! I don't know what she's got against Asians, but you should have heard her! I'm sure she's offended most of the staff in Davies Hospital by now, if she hadn't already. They're very racially integrated and she's just vicious! So, what's your news, Nick?"

"It pales in comparison, but I just signed the big contract I've been hoping for. There's this guy from back east who inherited tons of money, so he bought a winery he wants me to landscape. He's adding new buildings, including a huge tasting room and visitors' center. It's just south of St. Helena, over in the Napa Valley. I'm driving over there Thursday to have a look around and then I'll draw up some plans to show him. They should be ready for my crew to get started in about three or four weeks. Do you want to come and work for me this summer? I'll need to hire more people."

"That's great," Tim said, although he knew he was still in no shape to do heavy manual labor and the new job would keep Nick busy and the two of them apart more than ever. "It looks like I'll be going back to work at Arts in a couple of weeks."

"Good for you, Snowman! Are you sure you're feeling up to it?"

"I guess so..."

"Hey, I thought I'd drive down to the city tonight and take you out to dinner to celebrate my new contract... if you feel like it."

"Sure," Tim said. "You bet."

"Just name the place and make the reservations, okay? Surprise me. The sky's the limit. Anyplace except Orphan Andy's. We can go there for breakfast in the morning if you like. Hey, have you heard the latest news?"

"What news? I only glanced at the morning paper."

"No, it wouldn't have made the paper. It happened since then. I had the radio on in the office just before my client got here and they've found some more body parts."

"Really?"

"Yes, in San Francisco Bay."

"Whereabouts?"

"Pier 39," Nick said. "You know where the sea lions are?"

"Yeah, but I heard the sea lions all disappeared, went to Oregon or someplace."

"They did but they've all come back now, according to the guy on the radio. He said they were out there playing, tossing back and forth some things that were floating in the water. The tourists were taking pictures, as usual, and then a human leg landed up on the dock. One woman fainted and people started screaming when they realized the sea lions were tossing around body parts! Everyone had a camera, so there should be tons of pictures on the news later... *if* they dare to show them. Gross."

"Wow, I'll bet. I'll turn on the TV and see if there's any breaking news about it now."

"If not, it should be on the local news at five. According to the radio, they've found two legs, two arms with the hands missing—maybe one of them was the partial hand that Arturo and I found in the dumpster behind the restaurant—and a male torso, but no head. Some of the restaurants along there just closed up for the rest of the day. I guess nobody was hungry after witnessing that. I can see how it might kill your appetite."

"If those came from Hartford Street, they must have been pretty well decomposed by now. Gross is right!"

"They would have been, Snowman," Nick said, "but the body parts must have just been dumped there today because they were still frozen solid. That's why they were floating, I guess."

"More like an iceman than a snowman, huh?"

"Hey, I've got another call, but I should be in town by no later than seven if that's good for you."

"You bet. I guess there are several restaurants I can take off my list of where to eat tonight."

"Sorry, man... like I said, it's up to you. I don't care where we go. Surprise me. Anyplace you want, Snowman."

"After what you just told me, I'm thinking vegetarian at this point." Tim reached for the remote. "See you at seven."

"Later, Babe. I'll bring along my new wedlock and tie you up after dinner, okay?"

"You bet, stud," Tim hung up the phone and turned on the television. There was no breaking news, so he crawled under the top blanket on his bed and a nap seemed like just the right thing at the moment.

Tim's dream began as little more than glimpses of light like night scenes in a movie shot from the window of a fast-moving train. Then there was the cat. Bartholomew was licking Tim's face, kneading his paws into Tim's shoulder, telling him it was time. They were in his Aunt Ruth's apartment on Collingwood Street but Tim still lived there and Bartholomew did too. This was how dreams were. Tim had gotten used to the way familiar things changed form and time and space. He and the cat had never lived in that apartment at the same time. That meant he had to be dreaming and this might be one of those dreams like his grandmother had, the dreams that meant something.

The cat couldn't really speak, not even in his dream, but Tim heard the message loud and clear so he got up and put on his shoes. He looked at himself in the mirror and saw that he was wearing pajamas with cactus plants and donkeys and sombreros on them, the same pajamas he'd worn when he was a little boy.

He grabbed a jacket and walked out the door, headed down Castro Street in his little boy pajamas and a black leather jacket and the sneakers that he kept in his locker at the gym. They were good sneakers for working out, but not great sneakers to run in. Still, he knew he could run if he had to.

Tim started to laugh. Yes, he had to be dreaming! He would never go out in public dressed like this. He outgrew these pajamas before puberty, but they fit him great right now. Tim thought about the guys who walked around the neighborhood stark naked. That fad hadn't really caught on, maybe because it wasn't warm enough lately, but Tim might start a new trend. Everyone would start wearing pajamas in public soon, but on Castro Street the pajamas would come in leather... or denim... or Spandex.

When Tim got to the restaurant Artie was behind the bar and James was at the waiters' station. Tim walked past all the customers seated at the bar and no one turned around to look at his ridiculous outfit. People he knew were sitting there eating and Tim might as well have been invisible. He was glad no one laughed and pointed.

Tim went through the swinging doors to the kitchen where Jake loaded dinner plates up one arm. Arturo had his back to them and Jake didn't notice Tim either, so he kept on walking... out the back door. Nick was standing beside the dumpster holding a long tool like a shovel or a broom in both his hands. Nick didn't notice Tim either, so he walked up closer to find out what Nick was doing. The tool was a rake. Nick was stirring the dumpster with a garden rake. The dumpster was filled with human eyeballs in marinara sauce. All the irises were green, emerald green, the brightest green Tim had ever seen.

# Chapter 20

Ruth wanted nothing more than to get that horrible white box and its gruesome contents out of her apartment. She wanted to call Captain O'Sullivan right away, but Teresa insisted on calling Peter Parker, her new boyfriend, first. Ruth was ready to scream by the time she got him on the phone, but Teresa thought it would look better in the eyes of his superiors if Peter turned over this new evidence before anyone else could claim it.

The three of them sat around Ruth's kitchen table and Teresa answered most of his questions, which didn't take long. She was the one who had found the box, but she'd already told Peter nearly everything they knew on the phone.

Now Peter wasn't here as Teresa's new beau, but as Officer Parker. He handled the evidence with sterile latex gloves, put the threatening note, the white box with its crumpled newspapers and the pierced human nose in the zip-lock bag inside a larger evidence box to take with him back to the station. He agreed that there wasn't much likelihood of finding fingerprints besides those of Ruth and Teresa. They hadn't found prints at the meth lab on Hartford Street either, so there were none for comparisons. Whatever person or persons involved were no doubt just as careful as the police were.

"Shouldn't we call Captain O'Sullivan now?" Ruth asked Peter.

"No, Miss Taylor. Please, Ma-am. Let me handle it. He's finally got the day off today and I'd say he sure needs one. He's been in a nasty mood and snapping at everyone lately and I'd hate to disturb him and the Mrs. at home.

Ruth promised to keep her doors locked and Peter promised to have someone drive by the place regularly, just in case whoever threatened her decided to came back. Now that Peter Parker and Teresa were gone, Ruth felt more relieved than frightened to be alone. She picked up her coffee and took a sip but it was cold, so she dumped it and rinsed the cup in the sink.

Things seemed almost back to normal until Ruth sighed and took a deep breath. Something didn't smell right. The nose and the eyeball had been frozen solid and nobody had opened that zip-lock bag and let the smell out. There was no need. It was easy enough for her and Teresa to see what was inside once they'd read the note.

"Maybe I'm only imagining things, but some fresh air in here wouldn't hurt now, would it?" Ruth said out loud as she opened the back door and the kitchen window, even though the temperature was cool and the sky still overcast. The apartment felt much too quiet and lonely now that Officer Parker and Teresa had left. If the cat were home she could pretend to be talking to him, but under the circumstances she would just have to talk out loud to herself. "Oh, Bartholomew… you bad, bad boy! Where the heck did you disappear to this time?"

She heard a truck shift gears on the hill going up Castro Street, the pop-pop-pop of a motor scooter and the rattle of the garbage haulers from Sunset Scavengers. Most ground floor windows in San Francisco had bars on them, even in the nicest neighborhoods. Even without bars, the window only opened a few inches, just wide enough for the cat to climb back in. Ruth hoped so. She missed Bartholomew. When he did come home again she vowed to be especially nice to him and give him a special treat. He'd suffered through Dianne's visit just like the rest of them.

Ruth sat down again and called Sam's private number. She didn't want to alarm him, but he would be upset if he heard about the gruesome delivery on her doorstep from anyone else. If she told him first, he'd be able to hear the calmness in her voice and know that she was alright. Ruth heard a recorded voice instruct her to leave a message. Sam must be in a meeting with a client. Ruth took a deep breath and smiled. She'd always heard that smiling made one's *telephone voice* more pleasant.

"Hi Sam, it's me… Ruth. Please give me a call when you get this. There's been a rather nasty development on this end, I'm afraid, but I'm fine—really. I don't want to worry you, but I'd feel an awfully lot better if you could drive up this evening and maybe even spend the night here. Then I can tell you all about it in person. If I'm not home when you get this message, please try my cell phone. Thanks Sam."

She hung up and hoped that sounded okay. Now she was even more concerned about Bart than her own safety. If Sam knew about the threatening note, he would whisk her out of there. If she refused the safety of his house in Hillsborough, he would insist on taking her to a hotel. As much as she enjoyed room service and spa treatments and sweeping views of the city, there was no way Bartholomew could find her if she was ensconced in a suite at the Fairmont or the Mark Hopkins.

Ruth picked up one of the flyers she'd promised to bring to Arts. The photograph of this young man with or without the gold ring through his nostril would be of no use, now. She felt sick to think that the nose in the photograph and one of those once bright and lively emerald eyes had been right here on her kitchen table a few moments ago.

She reached for the phone and punched in the number at the bottom of the flyer. She wanted to do it quickly before she chickened out. The police should be notifying Patrick, she thought, but it would be better for him to hear the news from her, instead of from a total stranger. He was the one who made that remark about her seeming like somebody's mom. Even though she wasn't even Dianne's mother, she liked the idea of the kids in the neighborhood thinking of her that way. Some of them, no doubt, didn't have moms that were, to use Patrick's word, "cool."

Ruth was so used to leaving messages, she had no idea what she would say if a living person answered her call, so it came as a relief when a recording from E.T. clicked on. It didn't sound like Patrick's voice. It could have even been Darryl's. Ruth shuddered at the thought, but she wasn't sure how large an organization E.T. was or how often they changed their outgoing message. She tried to summon up a smile and the same calm voice she'd used when she called Sam:

"Hello... My name is Ruth Taylor and I'm trying to reach a young fellow named Patrick. I'm sorry I don't even remember his last name. I probably should, since we used to work together at Arts Bar and Restaurant on Castro Street, but anyway... This has to do with a friend of his and the flyers he gave me and... um... if he could please give me a call I'd sure appreciate it, okay? Thanks. Bye, now."

Ruth no sooner hung up than she had to call right back again because she'd forgotten to leave her number. This time she felt her voice quaver a little and it seemed that she must have sounded on the verge of tears, so she quickly left her cell phone number, her home phone, Sam's home number and even the telephone number at Arts, just to be on the safe side.

Her next call was to her old friend Cindy, Dianne's biological mother in Boston. She looked at the clock on the kitchen wall and it was barely noon, but Ruth got a bottle of white wine from the fridge and poured herself half a glass just to fortify her. It would be three hours later in Boston. This was the perfect time.

Ruth had never really believed this day would come. She'd grown so used to Dianne and the way things were that she had never taken the time to fully imagine this moment. It was just as well that she hadn't had time to dread it. Ruth always believed that the fear of something was usually worse than the "something" was.

Ruth tended to doodle when she was nervous. By the time she finally hung up the phone with Cindy, she had no idea how much time had passed, but the pad of paper under her hand was nearly full. Her mouth felt dry, so she took another sip of wine and emptied the glass. That was when she noticed that the bottle had mysteriously made its way from the refrigerator to the kitchen table and it was empty, too. It couldn't have been more than half full to begin with, could it?

Ruth was so dazed that she could barely remember the words she'd used to explain to Cindy what had happened. Maybe it was the wine, but the entire phone call seemed to have taken place outside of real time. Ruth was sure there had been no tears or raised voices. As the evening wore on and during the next few days the conversation would come back to her memory in bits and pieces like a dream. And in the coming months it would fade away as if it never took place.

Right now, at her kitchen table in Tim's old apartment on Collingwood Street, Ruth looked down at the yellow tablet that was filled with her own handwriting and indecipherable scribbles. There were Cindy's telephone numbers at home, plus her cell phone and office. There was a familiar address and zip code in Boston. Then it said:

Family:

Cindy - Mother - Ruth - Mother -
Dianne - Daughter -
Men -
Boys - Castro boys - Mom -

Crystal Methamphetamine
Speed - Tina
Kidney dialysis -
Kidneys, Livers, gizzards,
eyeballs - HANDS -
golden earrings -

Then there was a bunch of doodling Ruth couldn't make out... words... numbers... and what looked like a hand with a face behind it. That was it. A hand was covering a face, like Mai Ling's hand covering her face when she'd been so embarrassed about Nancy Kwan and Rene scolded her. What was Ruth thinking about that for? She had no idea.

The list began again:

Family:

Ruth & Dan Taylor
Dianne - daughter -
Friendship:
Cindy - Sister - Friend - Cindy -

Family:

Ruth Taylor - Sam Connor

Family:

The gay boys...
Nick & Tim -
Artie & Arturo -

Family:

Sam Connor's daughter -
Jane & Ben Larson and their children:
Sarah, the Magic Child -
Baby Samuel Timothy
Adam -

Ruth was still drawing circles and squiggles and loops in the margins as she re-read the page, but now she stopped. What was Adam's name doing there among Sam's family? She might have mentioned Tim to her old friend Cindy while she was doodling and talking on the phone. It wouldn't have been unusual to have talked about Tim and Nick in the same sentence. And it would have been natural for Cindy to ask if Ruth was seeing anyone, so Sam's name came up and therefore his daughter – "Jane & Ben" and their children. Where did Adam fit in, though?

Ruth felt a tingle like a cold finger down her spine and sat up very straight in her chair for a moment. It must be the wine. She wasn't used to drinking in the daytime. When she looked back down at the page, she noticed that Adam was followed by more names:

- Adam -
- Connie - Kyle - Anna - Mitchell -
- David - Randall and Rebecca -

Now she remembered that Randy and Becky were Cindy's twins. All these names were Cindy's children in order of age. Adam was the oldest. Ruth had seen their names and pictures in every Christmas card. Their hairstyles and clothing might have changed over the years, but Ruth thought she could recognize each and every one of them, even across a crowded airport lobby, even if their meeting was accidental. These were Dianne's real siblings; at least they were her half-brothers and sisters. They were more closely related to Ruth's daughter than she was.

The telephone rang and brought Ruth back to the present. "Tim!" she shouted, relieved to hear his voice, rather than Patrick calling back so soon, or even Sam. Tim would be reassuring to talk to, but mostly she just listened. "Yes, Tim... yes, I see. Yes, my line was busy... I'm sorry to worry you. I was talking to my old friend Cindy in Boston and also... No... I haven't seen any television news. Oh, my! Don't tell me they're already reporting on that box that came here..."

Ruth reached for the remote to turn on the portable TV set in the corner of the kitchen. "No, Tim... there doesn't seem to be anything on the local channels right now. On the radio? Nick did... I see. Down by the wharf there, huh?"

She listened to Tim tell her how happy he was that Nick was on his way down to celebrate a new contract by taking them out to dinner. "The box? Well, honestly, Tim, you haven't given me a chance. Teresa thought it was flowers at first, but there was a zip-lock bag inside with an eyeball and a nose with a gold ring and a note. They were frozen, too, or at least they had been. If they match the body parts in the bay and the things they found in the sewer pipes on Castro Street, then I guess all that's missing now is the head. But there were Polaroid pictures of it in the box. Do they still make Polaroids?"

Now she was afraid that Tim was getting excited and she hadn't meant to upset him. "No, Tim, there's no need for you to rush over here. I'm fine, really. The police have already come and gone and taken everything away. There's a patrol car practically circling my block. I couldn't feel safer. Besides, I've already called Sam to come and spend the night. He's probably on his way right now."

Ruth wished Sam was on his way this fast. She felt lonely in her kitchen all of a sudden and there was a cold draft with the window open, but she didn't want Bartholomew to come home and not be able to get inside. Where was that cat?

"I could come over if you want me to and wait for Sam with you." Tim's words through the telephone were tempting.

"No, no… you just give Nick my love and you two boys have a lovely evening. I'll call you on your cell if anything else comes up, okay? I promise. Don't forget to carry it with you. Bye, now…"

Ruth didn't want to lie to her nephew. She *had* called Sam. That part was true, but she didn't know when he would get her message and whether he could come to the city, much less spend the night with her, unless she told him the whole truth. Still, there was nothing Tim could do about the situation.

Where was Bartholomew? Of all the times when she could use a big furry cat to hold and cuddle, this was one. There was no reason for him to run off today. Dianne was still a few blocks away in Davies hospital. She wasn't around to torment either one of them.

Ruth walked up the hallway to her living room. The western sky looked clear as a bell. There wouldn't be any fog tonight and even though it wasn't very warm outside, it was too nice an afternoon to stay cooped up in here, waiting for something to happen.

She picked up her purse and her cell phone and locked the back door. She even locked the deadbolt on the front door on her way out of her apartment. She often got lazy about locking that one, although she made a big show of locking it once for Dianne on the first day she arrived. She supposed Dianne would be leaving soon, now that the medical tests were back and the truth was out. Dianne wouldn't waste time looking for a kidney here, now that she knew her real mother and siblings lived in Boston and not in San Francisco. Ruth stood inside the gate and waited to see if a police car really would come by.

It seemed like a long time before any car at all drove up Collingwood Street. There was a single man driving it. He wore his collar turned up and his hat pulled down. Maybe it was an unmarked police car. They probably wouldn't want to be too obvious.

Ruth just couldn't wait any longer. She was tired of waiting. Now that she had a plan in mind she felt more in control, more like her old self again. And as soon as she stepped out into the fresh air she felt even better. She wanted to find her cat and she had a pretty good idea where to look for him this time.

# Chapter 21

The word spread quickly through Davies Hospital that a wicked witch was residing on the fourth floor. Dianne's acid tongue was nastier than any storybook villain. Lab technicians, office workers, even ambulance drivers who had no business on that floor could be seen sneaking past her room to see if the patient in Room #490 could really breathe fire.

No one might have been brave enough to go near her, but a couple of gay male nurses who patronized Arts Bar and Restaurant on Castro Street had recognized Tim and Ruth when they emerged from her room unharmed. They spread the word to their co-workers, many of whom thought Tim was cute.

The sedative they'd put into Dianne's IV kept her unconscious well past lunchtime, so that meant one less meal for her to complain about. When she finally did come around, Dianne decided to leave the hospital immediately. She ripped the IV out of her arm, got dressed and stepped onto the elevator before anyone knew she was awake. No one would have dared to stop her anyway.

Dianne was disgusted that she'd wasted time and money coming to San Francisco. What was she thinking? The sedative was wearing off as she tried to remember why—besides a kidney—the idea had occurred to her in the first place. Her marriage was floundering, but that was nothing new. As her husband's "business trips" grew longer and more frequent, Dianne had grown tired of sitting home with nothing to do but touch up her nails and argue with the help. She could only spend so many hours in church meetings or ooh-ing and aah-ing over porcelain figurines or stuffing envelopes for Christian political candidates, but where did she have to go?

San Francisco was not the answer. Her first choice would have been to visit her *father* in Minneapolis. He might have been willing to part with a kidney. She'd always been Dan Taylor's "little girl," but it was impossible to reach him lately. He'd created an army of secretaries and receptionists to guard against any reminders of his past. When Dianne decided on San Francisco instead, she thought it smarter to forge ahead without even calling first. What else could her boring little mother have to do than welcome her long lost daughter with open arms?

"Harrumph!" Dianne opened the gate on Collingwood Street. She hadn't counted on her own mother being an imposter! And she could hardly believe that drab woman who'd raised her, that simple Midwestern housewife had now somehow managed to snag herself a millionaire with a mansion in the suburbs of San Francisco.

Dianne hadn't counted on coming face to face with her cousin Tim, either. As far as she was concerned, when people ran away to San Francisco, they should disappear for good. If anything positive had come of all this, it was finding out that she wasn't related to that smart-mouthed pervert after all.

It was even worse to discover that she was related to a bunch of Jews, but she needed them for the time being. She would have to try to be pleasant enough to get a kidney out of one of her step-siblings and then she could shun them. She could spend the rest of her life pretending they never existed and nobody would have to know that she wasn't born a Protestant.

Dianne had trouble opening the deadbolt lock on the apartment door. Ruth never used it unless she planned to be gone for a while, which suited Dianne just fine. She wanted to be alone, to soak in a hot tub and get the hospital smell off her, then pack her bags and get out of here once and for all.

"Do you need some help there?" Dianne heard a voice behind her. It was the upstairs neighbor, that sickening freak named Marsha who used to be a boy. Dianne cringed at the thought of spending one more night in this God-forsaken place. She could picture a circus with its sideshow entertainers lined up and down both sides of Castro Street, including her former "cousin" Tim. She imagined the garish signs behind them: *See the Amazing "Half-man/Half-woman"* or *"Alligator Lady and her husband, the Rubber Man"* or *"Watch the Sword-Swallowing Boy"* spelled out on gaudy canvasses and billowing in the fog.

"I can get it myself!" she snapped at Marsha. Thank goodness the deadbolt finally turned before Dianne went insane. Marsha flitted up the stairs to his/her own apartment and Dianne could have sworn she smelled popcorn, salted peanuts and zebra shit. She heard the distant trumpeting of an elephant in the squeal of someone's brakes on the steep Collingwood hill. Lions roared in the wind outside.

Dianne set her purse on a kitchen chair and looked at the note-pad that Ruth had left behind. Most of it was gibberish, a bunch of squiggles and doodles and then she saw the name of Cindy and realized that this list of names and telephone numbers in Boston might come in handy. She tore the page from the note pad, folded it and dropped it into her purse. Next she called the airport while the bathtub filled. She would catch the next available flight to just about anywhere in order to get out of this hellhole.

Ruth didn't even stop at Arts. She figured that if someone was out to get her, he would look in one of two places first—her apartment or the restaurant. Her apartment seemed a little safer than a public place, but it felt too stifling to stay there. And if she went to the restaurant she'd not only make a target of herself but also risk the safety of the customers and her co-workers. Besides, Ruth was worried about Bartholomew, so she tried to think like a cat.

She crossed Castro Street and kept going on 19th, turned left at Hartford and hoped she could remember which building it was where Bart hid out before. Last time she and Amanda Musgrove had approached it from the back side. She needn't have worried. A row of avocado green refrigerators stood on the sidewalk out front—exactly like the one in the photograph. Their doors had been removed so that children couldn't crawl inside and get trapped. The freezer side was just wide enough for a human head. She also noticed that there were only five refrigerators and there were six apartments.

A car pulled out of the driveway, nearly hit her, and sped north in a hurry, close enough for her to get a glimpse of the driver and the passenger. Ruth might not have been able to swear to it in a court of law, but she guessed that the driver was Al Molino, the owner of the card shop next door to Arts. The passenger was his brother Ed from Chicago, who had recently bought this building. Or they could have been the other way around. They weren't twins, but they looked enough alike to confuse anyone at a glance.

"Good, that means nobody's home," Ruth thought to herself. Then she wondered why the Molino brothers weren't in jail. At least Ed, the one who had his name on the deed to this building, should have been in some kind of trouble for allowing a methamphetamine lab in the basement.

The gate was held open with a single copy of the "Watchtower" magazine. It was the same issue Amanda used before, with the shepherd on the cover and his flock of sheep on a hillside under a bright yellow sun in a deep blue sky. Ruth also remembered that Amanda put both copies back in her purse when they were finished here the other day. They'd left a stack of Bay Area Reporters in the front hallway, but there was no sign of them now.

Ruth stepped inside and placed the religious tract back where she found it. She had a superstitious feeling about not wanting to move anything. Ruth couldn't imagine why

Amanda had come back here alone, but it was strange to see the gate held open just like last time. She walked down the long, dark hallway to the rear of the building. The room where she'd first discovered her cat was empty now. The cans of paint thinner were gone too and Ruth noticed a row of water heaters against the wall, but they must have been there all along.

"Bartholomew! Here, kitty, kitty, kitty. Bartholomew! Are you hiding from me, you naughty boy? Here, baby..." Ruth's voice echoed off the walls in the empty room. She thought she heard a cat's cry in the distance, but it could have been coming from another house down the block or it might have only been her imagination.

She pressed the secret panel and entered the room where she and Amanda had discovered the illegal laboratory. It was empty. The vials and beakers were gone. The hot plates and trash cans and coffee filters had all been removed. The tables were gone too, even the one where she'd found Bartholomew licking the bloody meat cleaver. Ruth hadn't thought to bring a flashlight, but she didn't need one. Last time the windows were covered over with cardboard, but now the sunlight shafted through the dusty air.

It looked like someone had attached a high-powered nozzle to a garden hose and flushed everything out of the room. Exhaust vents for three clothes dryers lined the wall along with plumbing for a row of washing machines. There was nothing sinister about a utility room. Ruth felt silly for having been so frightened.

"Meow!" It was loud and clear this time, but it came from somewhere above her. Ruth ran up the stairs to the first floor of flats. Their lay-outs were a mirror image of each other, running from the front to the back of the building. Both kitchen doors stood wide open, one halfway off its hinges like it had been broken in. Ruth stuck her head inside each apartment and called, "Bart! Here boy! Are you in here, baby? Bartholomew!"

She climbed another flight of stairs. The apartments on the middle floor were being renovated. One had ladders and drop cloths, roller pans and paintbrushes everywhere. The other smelled of fresh paint and there was a wide-belt sander standing in the middle of the floor in the second room. A chandelier hung from the center of the ceiling, wrapped in an old pillowcase to keep the sawdust off.

Ruth wondered if the Molino brothers were doing the renovation work themselves. Maybe they had just run out of something and were off on a quick trip to a lumberyard or paint store. They might come back any minute and Ruth was getting nervous again. Maybe Amanda had only taken one of the "Watchtower" papers with her and dropped the other one. Maybe Ed Molino was out on bail. Maybe one of the old refrigerators had already been hauled away.

Ruth leaned on a kitchen counter beside an open window while a dozen "maybes" spun through her mind. She felt dizzy and she craved a cigarette, even though she hadn't smoked one in twenty years. "Meow," came from the airshaft beside the pantry. Her cat must be directly above her. She didn't call him this time. Something didn't sound right. Ruth tiptoed up the stairs to the top floor and found another pair of doors standing open.

The apartment on the north side was in worse shape than those on the first floor. This one was empty of furniture and appliances. The wallpaper was peeling and holes between rooms looked like someone went crazy with an axe. Huge streaks of bright graffiti jumped out at Ruth everywhere she looked. One room was painted black with splotches of fluorescent Day-Glo paint, someone's LSD nightmare of a terrifying night sky sprayed across a cracked ceiling.

Ruth thought she heard the cat in the apartment on the north side, but there was no sign of him. She tried to remember details of the day she was here with Amanda. This was the apartment where the man was drying his head with the towel—Al Molino, they'd assumed—and he had yelled down to "Eddie" that he'd come too early. Now Ruth saw a rusty teakettle on the front burner of a filthy gas stove. Its yellow finish was chipped in several places and it had a broken handle. The sink overflowed with dirty unmatched dishes, most of them cracked. Ruth could stock a better kitchen at any thrift store in town. Then she turned around and froze at the sound of a motor. The Kenmore avocado green side-by-side refrigerator/freezer was near enough to touch, but there was no way Ruth was going any closer.

She hurried past the dining room that held nothing but cardboard boxes and a drop-leaf table. She passed two closed doors on her left and came to the front room with a broken-down green plaid sofa and a coffee table covered with old *Hustler* magazines. In the bay window an overstuffed armchair had springs and stuffing poking out. Near the window a dead ficus tree stood in a clay pot full of cigarette butts. "Bartholomew?" Ruth barely dared to whisper. "I know you're here somewhere. Come out, boy. Where are you hiding?"

Ruth saw movement out of the corner of her eye. The doorway swung all the way open and she nearly screamed at the silhouette of a man. He was holding her cat in both his hands. "Captain O'Sullivan! Oh my goodness... I'm so glad to see you. I've been looking everywhere for my cat and you've found him at last. Thank you so much. What a relief! I almost didn't recognize you out of your uniform. I don't know why I'm so jumpy today, but I've been searching all through this creepy old apartment building. Say... maybe you'd know why the Molino brothers aren't in jail. I'm sure I saw them driving off a little while ago. Wait a minute... I thought Officer Parker said you had the day off and you were home with—"

"Then I take it this is your missing cat, Miss Taylor?"

"Yes, that's my naughty boy. He ran away again and I found him over here in this building the last time. He doesn't care for my daughter at all. I mean... my houseguest. Come here now, Bart..."

Bartholomew jumped out of the policeman's arms and into hers. When he did, Ruth saw what the cat had been concealing n Captain O'Sullivan's right hand. It was a gun, a black Beretta. O'Sullivan pointed it at Ruth and nothing stood in his way this time.

# Chapter 22

Dianne soon discovered that there were any number of flights back to Texas if she didn't mind going by way of Chicago or Denver or LAX. She didn't care about the cost, as long as she got out of San Francisco as soon as she could. She was ready to hire a private plane if need be. Her first priority would be to get back to Texas, see her doctor and find out how long before she'd have to start dialysis and/ or get a transplant. The less time she had, the sooner she'd have to travel to Boston and ingratiate herself with a bunch of strangers who were blood relation, whether she liked that fact or not. She dreaded having to be polite to a bunch of people who weren't even Christians, but she had to do what she had to do.

Whichever flight she took, she still had a couple of hours to kill. She turned on the faucet in the bathroom and continued packing while the tub filled. The bath helped a little; Dianne didn't feel as sticky as she did in that horrible hospital bed. To her delicate sensibilities, the clothes she wore back to Ruth's apartment were so wrinkled and stale she was tempted to throw them away, even though this was one of her favorite summer dresses. She found a plastic garbage bag under the sink and packed up everything that hadn't been laundered. Thank goodness her maid back home knew how to handle fine fabrics. Dianne saw to that when she hired her, even though she was disappointed with the woman's English.

While packing, Dianne came to two unpleasant realizations. First, she had no one to help her carry all her things out to the car. At least it was still parked on Collingwood, right where she'd left it, and hadn't been towed. She knew there wouldn't be any problem on the other end, whether her husband or children where around or not. She could simply call home and have one of the Mexicans bring a car to meet her.

Even at SFO, she didn't foresee any trouble. Dianne knew the value of dressing well and flashing money around. It didn't matter how many of her jewels were real or how much of her money she was actually going to part with. Menial laborers always snapped to attention when they thought they were getting a good tip. Dianne was known to wrap a one-dollar bill around a little green booklet full of prayers and Bible verses. By the time the suckers realized how little Dianne had given them, she was well on her way. She always got a laugh out of that trick and they could curse her all they wanted once she was gone.

Her second unpleasant realization was that she couldn't find the keys to her rented town car. She was sure they would turn up somewhere in this mess, but as she filled her bags and the piles of things around them disappeared, her hopes dimmed.

Dianne went to the kitchen where she'd left her purse on a chair. A foghorn sounded in the distance and a siren screamed by, followed by another and another—fire trucks or ambulances going down Castro Street. She slammed the kitchen window shut to try to block out those depressing sounds. As far as she was concerned, this entire revolting neighborhood could burn to the ground. It would be an improvement.

Dianne jumped when Ruth's wall phone rang in the kitchen, but Dianne didn't dare answer it. Maybe it was the hospital calling Ruth to tell her that her daughter had escaped.

Dianne laughed and listened as the answering machine came on and recorded a young man's voice leaving a message:

*"Hi Ruth… this is Patrick at the E.T. hot line. I'm returning your call. You said you might know something about a friend of mine. I guess you must have meant mean Darryl. I'm home now. It's the same number, if you get this before I reach you. I just tried to leave a message on your cell phone too, but I'm not sure if it took. I might have gotten cut off. Anyway, I hope you remembered to put up those flyers I gave you at the restaurant. Let me know if you need any more. I'll try calling you there next. Bye…"*

The contents of Dianne's purse clattered out across the kitchen table. Those car keys had to be in here somewhere. She put each item back inside, but the only keys were the set Ruth had loaned her to the apartment on Collingwood. Then she remembered where the car keys had to be. The day she fainted in the restaurant she'd been searching through her purse for her wallet. She was trying to pay for a glass of wine before that chubby old bartender—what was his name —Marty? Barty?—took the money that the black guy was offering. She certainly didn't want to be indebted to him!

The car keys could have fallen on the floor during all the commotion when she fell or while the paramedics were taking her out to the ambulance. She didn't remember any of it, but that was the only logical explanation for what must have happened. Whoever gathered up her things must have failed to put the keys back in her bag. Now she would have to make one more trip to that restaurant, just when she'd hoped to avoid ever setting foot on Castro Street again.

She'd planned on just sending Ruth a breezy note when she got home. Even though the woman wasn't Dianne's mother, she wouldn't want Ruth to think she had no class. She might even send along a small gift to thank her for her hospitality. Dianne had duplicates of some of her lesser-valued figurines that she used for such occasions. Sometimes they would set a person with half-way decent taste on the road to a lifetime of joy when they discovered the value of collectibles.

Dianne looked around Ruth's kitchen again and had grave doubts about her taste. A big tacky rainbow flag hung down from one corner of the room and beneath it on the wall there was a calendar of bare-chested men, for heaven's sake.

It looked like getting out of town wasn't going to be as simple a break as she'd hoped, but she wouldn't have to send anything if she said good-bye in person. Dianne decided that was the least she could do, since the woman raised her, after all.

Tim watched Nick stir the eyeballs in the dumpster with a rake. Nick's shirt was off now, so Tim could watch the smooth muscles play across his back and shoulders and arms. The hair on Nick's arms was already blond, but so many years of working out in the sun had bleached them white. The hair on Nick's forearms thinned to a trace and disappeared altogether before it reached his smooth round biceps, then grew again in a slightly darker patch under each armpit. Tim wanted to reach out and touch the palms of his hands to Nick's flesh, but when he tried he came awake... holding his hands above the bed.

Tim rolled over and punched the pillow, then fell back to sleep and into another dream. This time he was right here in his bedroom. Nick was here too... and Jason. At first Tim thought Nick and Jason were fighting over him, but they weren't fighting. They were having sex with each other, sweat pouring off both of them while Tim was on the sidelines... ignored. Tim was hurt and at the same time he was furious at himself for feeling jealous over a dead man. Besides, he and Jason had been lovers too, at least for a while.

But they didn't know each other while Jason was alive... or did they? Nick's grandparents lived in this apartment while Nick was growing up and Jason lived downstairs until he was murdered... there. Nick claimed he didn't know Jason then, but was that possible?

Even if Nick and Jason had hooked up, it wouldn't have been here in Nick's grandparents' home. It would have been downstairs in Jason's apartment... or someplace else. Arms and legs flew everywhere. Nick and Jason were flying around the room and now so were eyeballs and severed heads and bits of ice, everything dripping with blood. Then the naked men in Tim's dream were no longer Nick and Jason. They were strangers tearing each other apart.

The phone rang until it woke Tim. He had turned off the answering machine because in case Nick called he didn't want to sleep through the four rings and make him leave a message. Now he reached for the phone in a daze after eight rings.

"Hey Tim, it's Patrick. I almost gave up on you. I hope I'm not disturbing anything."

"No, that's okay. What's up?"

"You sound sleepy. Did I wake you?"

"What time is it? I guess so, but that's okay, really. I've got to get up and take a shower anyway. I'm going out to dinner with Nick later. I thought this might be him. I guess I was having a bad dream."

"Oh... sorry, well the reason I'm calling is because your Aunt Ruth left a message on the E.T. hotline. It's my number, actually, but she didn't know that. It's the number that's on that flyer with Darryl's picture and stuff. Her message sounded like she might know something about him, but I called her at home and on her cell phone and I left messages on both of them. I called Arts and they haven't seen her either, but they said Nick's grandmother had been in there looking for her, too. I thought maybe she was at your place, but I guess not if you're sleeping. Do you have any idea where she is?"

"Um... Patrick..." Tim tried to stall for time to think. He was still half asleep. His Aunt Ruth had said something about a package left on her doorstep, but he'd been so busy telling her about the body parts in the bay and Nick coming to town for dinner tonight that he wasn't paying as much attention as he should have. Now he felt guilty. He should have been worried about his Aunt Ruth, not Patrick. When she'd told him the police had already been there, Tim figured the situation was under control.

"I don't know what to tell you, Patrick. She called earlier and said the police had come by her place, but she told me not to worry. She didn't mention you or anything. I'm sorry I can't be more help, but she's not here, anyway… in answer to your question."

"Okay, Tim. Sorry to bother you."

"That's okay…" Tim hated to think it might be Patrick's missing friend being tossed about by the sea lions at Pier 39, but he didn't want to repeat second-hand gossip. He wished his Aunt Ruth were there right now. She'd be better at handling a situation like this than Tim ever was.

"Hey Patrick?" The phone line had been quiet so long that Tim thought he might have hung up.

"Yeah, Tim?"

"I was talking to Arturo the other day and he wondered if you wanted some shifts at Arts. They need a fill-in waiter for vacations and I'm not sure whether I'm ready to go back to work quite yet."

"Maybe… yeah, that might be a good idea. I could use the money, but first I need to find Darryl. I'll stop by there and talk to them. Maybe I'll go today and see if your Aunt Ruth has shown up there, too. Thanks, Tim."

As soon as Tim hung up the phone with Patrick he called Nick and left a message:

"Hey Nick… if I'm not home when you get into town, come and meet me at Arts, okay? We need to talk."

Tim figured that the restaurant would be the most likely place for his Aunt Ruth to show up, unless she was with Sam. He might be taking her to some fancy place to eat or to another luxury hotel. Tim thought about calling Hillsborough, but she'd already told him that Sam was coming into the city this evening, so why would she go there?

Tim's nightmares made him even more uneasy than his conversation with Patrick. Something didn't feel right and Tim didn't want to sit here waiting for more phone calls, more questions, or more bad news. He took a quick shower and pulled on a T-shirt, a pair of jeans and some sneakers. He could get dressed again later for dinner with Nick if they went someplace nice. He still hadn't thought about where he wanted to go or made any reservations.

Tim sat down at the bar and ordered a beer from Artie, who was too busy on the phone to answer any questions. "Ach! All the reservations are for early seating. Everyone in the Castro wants to have dinner before the premiere of that new David Weissman documentary at the Castro Theatre."

"What time is the movie?"

"7:15... I don't know why they have to make it so early."

"They'll probably do a Q and A afterward, don't you think?" But Artie was already reaching to answer the phone again. Tim had barely taken a sip of his beer when the door flew open and Dianne waltzed in looking none the worse for her hospital stay.

"Hello, Dianne," Artie said. "How are you feeling? I didn't know you were out of the hospital already. Are you looking for your mother?"

"If I was looking for my mother, I'd have to be in Boston right now! I'm looking for my stupid car keys! This is the only place they could possibly be! Did anyone turn them in?"

Artie's brow furrowed as he hung up the phone and turned toward Tim. "What's your Aunt Ruth doing in Boston? I wish someone had told me about this. Arturo and I have tickets to the symphony tomorrow night, but if Ruth is in Boston... wait a minute. If you knew she was in Boston, why did you come in here looking for her?"

"She's not in Boston, Artie," Tim explained. "Aunt Ruth isn't Dianne's real mother."

"What? Oh, damn! There's the phone again. Arts! Artie speaking... yes... two for six o'clock... no, Tim isn't back at work yet, but I can make a note to put you in Jake's section or James'? What's the name? Nelson, party of two at six o'clock with James… okay, we'll see you then… Now, what did you say, Tim?"

"David Weissman might be doing a Q & A after the film."

"No, not that, you ninny! About your Aunt Ruth!?"

"She's not Dianne's real mother."

"What? How long have you known about this? Why the secrecy?"

"Dianne and I both just found out about it today. It's kind of a long story, Artie, and maybe it'd be better if you asked her yourself sometime…"

"Well… Mrs. Musgrove was here looking for your Aunt Ruth too, but that was over an hour ago. She said she'd stop back in later, but so far there's been no sign of her returning. I haven't seen Ruth today at all and—"

"I said I was looking for my car keys, Farty!" Dianne interrupted. "Do you have a 'lost and found' department here or don't you?"

"Why, yes," Artie ignored her rude slip of the tongue and reached under the counter for a heavy cardboard box that—according to its faded printing—had once held Budweiser beer. "Anything that gets turned in usually ends up in this old beer case. You're welcome to look through it. Oh damn, there's the phone again!"

Dianne pulled open the flaps and tore through a mess of sunglasses, cheap cigarette lighters, dusty baseball caps, pillboxes, and empty wallets. "Aha! Here they are! Now I can get out of this godforsaken town. If that woman you all thought was my mother shows up, tell her goodbye for me, please."

"I know!" Tim had an idea. "If Nick's grandmother was here and she said she'd return, she must be investigating that house out in back. I'll bet Aunt Ruth is looking for Bartholomew again and that's the last place he was hiding, so I wouldn't be surprised if Aunt Ruth ran into Mrs. Musgrove and they're probably…"

"You mean that mangy old cat of hers?" Dianne asked.

"Oh, Dianne… I'd better go with you," Tim said. "You'll never find it. We can cut through the back door. It'll be closer that way to go out through the kitchen and down the driveway past the dumpsters. Oh, wait a minute. Now I've got a phone call. This might be Nick."

"Nevermind!" Dianne looked at her watch. "I still have an hour to kill. You take your phone call. I'll go and I'll find her and I'll say my own good-byes."

Dianne dropped the car keys into her shoulder bag and disappeared through the swinging back doors toward the kitchen. Tim and Artie heard the back door of the building slam shut a moment later, just as Patrick came in through the front door from Castro Street.

# Chapter 23

Ruth felt as if she'd been hypnotized by the gun in her face, a standard police-issue .40-caliber Beretta. She'd never seen a gun up so close before and she found it rather pretty, actually. Ruth couldn't have known it was the same gun that had been reported missing a couple of months ago when an anti-war rally at the Civic Center got out of hand.

"Poor Captain O'Sullivan," she thought to herself, "what an unhappy life he must have led to have reached this point." She didn't make a sound, of course, not even a whimper. She just stared at the gun, so black and sleek and functional. It said "Beretta" right there on the side, as well as "USA" and a bunch of numbers Ruth could almost make out without her reading glasses because it was so close to her face. It was a work of art, really… a piece of sculpture.

Time stood still in Ruth's dazed condition. She thought back to when Tim's father bought him a toy gun one Christmas when he was a little boy. She didn't like her brother-in-law encouraging Tim to play with guns, even though it was only a toy. It looked nothing like this one. Ruth was happy when Tim showed no interest in it. Ruth and Dan bought him a telescope that year, which he loved. He spent as much time spying on the neighbors as he did stargazing, though.

"Get in there!" Captain O'Sullivan's shout nudged Ruth back to the present, but only briefly. Had she always reacted to danger by going numb? She thought back to a summer night when she was a girl. A tornado ripped through their neighborhood in Minneapolis. Ruth remembered it like yesterday, the family huddled in the cellar—Ruth and her sister Betty and their parents—until it arrived with the roar and clatter of a freight train lumbering through the attic. After the monster was gone, they fell asleep on a pile of old blankets. When they emerged into the crisp light of morning, the garage was gone and so was their father's car. All that was left was a clean slab of concrete, as if it had always been so.

"Now!" He poked the gun barrel at her ribs through her thin blue cotton blouse, forcing Ruth to step inside the darkened bedroom to get away from the cold steel. The door slammed shut, blocking out any light from the hallway. Tattered curtains draped the windows, but even without them the light would have been dim. The building next door was less than a foot away. Ruth's eyes adjusted enough to make out a sagging mattress and box spring in one corner. Half a dozen oak chairs matched the dining room set she had passed in the other room.

Ruth saw a figure seated in one of the chairs. "Amanda!" Ruth made out the nose, eyes and forehead of the old woman. Her black scarf was wound around her head to gag her mouth and it was tied in knots in the back, but she was alive.

Dianne walked around the dumpsters behind Arts in shoes that were much too dressy for her surroundings. Whoever hauled out the trash must have lousy aim. Otherwise, someone ought to write a pointed letter to the garbage company that made this mess when they collected on this route. There was no excuse not to take pride in your job, no matter how menial. That's what Dianne always told the people who did her dirty work.

The single door in the back of the building was locked, so she headed down the driveway toward the front. A religious tract had been used to keep the gate open. Dianne bent down to admire the picture of Jesus and the sheep, but it was too dirty to pick it up. The place was being renovated, judging from the old appliances on the sidewalk and sawdust footprints everywhere. None of the doorbells had names in the spaces beside them, so she didn't bother trying to ring any of them.

Dianne couldn't imagine why Ruth would be looking for her cat back here. If the building wasn't occupied, there wouldn't be anyone feeding him or even any food scraps for him to eat. She also couldn't imagine why any living creature would want to catch its own food when it could relax in a sunny window and get three square meals a day—catered—but if ever a cat was stupid enough, Bartholomew would be the one.

"Mother?" Dianne yelled without thinking. She'd used the word "mother" for years, out of habit, but it was one she would soon break. As she started up the stairs, she yelled at the top of her lungs, "Hello! Anybody home?"

Ruth cocked her head at the sound of Dianne's voice and tried to move, but her gag only tightened when she did. Captain O'Sullivan stood across from his captives and laughed. "Now it looks like we've got three nosy women to dispose of. Some people just don't know when to mind their own business. I warned that boy with the ring in his nose to stay away from here too, but he didn't listen. Now he's spread out in pieces all over town. Maybe I didn't give him as clear a message as I did you, Miss Taylor, when I dropped off his nose at your place." O'Sullivan took a few steps toward the door and turned the knob, letting it swing part way open. "We might as well make the little lady feel welcome."

Bartholomew screamed a loud "Meow!" from his hiding place under the table and ran toward the open door, but O'Sullivan caught the cat with his foot and kicked. Bartholomew flew in an arc across the room and landed in the closet with a loud screech. O'Sullivan slammed the closet door shut and snarled, "I hope she's a cat-lover."

"What's going on?" Dianne yelled from the top of the stairs. She stepped through the bedroom's open doorway, whipped the sunglasses off her face and let them dangle on her fingertips a moment til they fell to the floor.

"We've been waiting for you, sweetheart. Now, you just drop that purse the same way you dropped those sunglasses and then you can have a seat right over here. I've got this chair all warmed up for you. Come on... nice and easy, now." He rubbed his crotch. "When Al and Eddie get back there'll be one lady for each of us. I'll pick you for myself, honey, and those other two can draw straws for the old broad or the nosy gold-digging bitch."

Dianne moved the fingertips of her left hand to the straps of her purse on her right shoulder. She had already slipped her right hand inside while the light from the hallway blinded the three of them who'd been waiting in the dark.

"That's it, lady. Drop the purse right there on the floor. You just do what you're told and then you and me will have a real nice time before we're through. What have you got in that big old purse, the kitchen sink? That's the biggest damned purse I ever..."

When Dianne's shoulder bag fell to the floor the rest of them caught the glint of a dainty silver revolver. Its ivory handle rested in the palm of her hand as she squeezed the trigger and shot Captain O'Sullivan straight through his filthy mouth. When he landed at her feet she shot him twice more, once through each eyeball.

"So, Artie... when do you need me to come back to work?" Patrick asked. "I could use some shifts here at the restaurant, I guess. I'm pretty broke these days. It's really nice of you guys to want me to come back and it would be a—" He and Tim were sitting together at the bar when Patrick's rambling was punctuated by the distant sound of three distinct shots coming from the direction of Hartford Street.

"What was that?" Tim interrupted.

"It sounded like a car backfiring to me," Patrick said. "I used to have a car that did that all the time. I got rid of it. It was in the shop more than it was on the street and I couldn't afford to keep putting money into it. How's Jason's old red Thunderbird running these days? That was always a great car."

Arturo heard the shots too. "We can talk about the schedule later, when everyone's here, but I don't think that was a car backfiring. Those sounded like gunshots to me."

Tim could only imagine that those three shots meant three victims—his Aunt Ruth, Nick's grandmother and Dianne, that nasty woman he'd grown up believing was his cousin. "I'm gonna go see what's going on out back. If Dianne found Aunt Ruth and the cat, they should have come back by now. If Bartholomew is hiding back there, Dianne will only scare him away again."

"Wait, Tim," Patrick said, "I'm coming with you."

Tim didn't wait for Patrick, but headed toward the swinging kitchen doors to go out the back way. "Artie, if we're not back in ten minutes or if you hear any more gunshots, call the police… right away!"

Dianne picked her purse up off the floor and blew on her gun, just as gently as if she were blowing out a single candle on a birthday cake. "I'll let this little baby cool down on the drive to the airport. And then she'll go back in my big pink suitcase before I check my bags. She always travels in her own special hiding place, my trusty little girl." Dianne brought the barrel of the gun to her lips and gave it a kiss before she dropped it back inside her purse. "I don't want any of those security retards they hire to work the x-ray machine manhandling me. I can tell they always want to."

Ruth tried to speak from behind her gag and Dianne started to loosen it, but changed her mind. "I know you ladies might find this hard to understand, but I just realized you're gonna have to wait for someone else to untie you. I just can't do it yet."

Dianne scowled. "Yuck, will you look at that! Now I'll have to change again before I go to the airport. That fool's brains are spattered all over my new shoes. Augh! There's some on my skirt, too."

Ruth tried to bite through her gag and scream, but all she could do was rock back and forth in the chair on the warped wooden floor of this old room. Dianne said, "The sound of those gunshots should bring you some help in no time, but I need a little head start before anyone gets here. If the cops come first and find out I've killed one of their cronies, they'll want to ask all sorts of stupid questions. He was a scumbag and he deserved what he got. Sorry, ladies, but I can't bear to spend one more night in this horrible city. It's worse than Sodom and Gomorrah rolled into one. If I ever come to California again it'll be too soon."

Dianne glanced at her watch. "If I hurry, I can turn in the car at the airport and be on the next flight to Houston. I'll be in the air before they even finish grilling you two. Then I'll see my own doctor and fly on to Boston eventually to look up the Jews. By the way, Mother… I mean Ruth… I found that piece of paper with their phone numbers on it. Now I can just hope and pray that one of them will be a match and can give me a new kidney."

Dianne picked up a torn pillowcase from the bed and tried to wipe the bloody viscera from her shoes, but it was no use. "Darn it! I don't know if this will ever come out. These are suede, too. Anyway… Ruth—I can't call you 'Mother' anymore after you lied to me all these years—I suppose you did the best you could, but it was still a lie! Now that I've saved your life and killed this stupid turkey before he could rape me and shoot the both of you, I hope we can consider ourselves even-Steven, okay?"

Dianne picked up her purse and sunglasses and stepped out into the hallway, but stuck her head back in the room for a moment. "Just one more thing… you should consider going to church more often than at Christmas and Easter, if you bother to go at all. You can pray for my eternal soul and for my kidneys at the same time. And you can give thanks that us Texas gals carry guns and vote for politicians that never stand in the way of the NRA. B-bye, now..."

# Chapter 24

"I can't get Mrs. Musgrove's gag untied!" Patrick yelled at Tim. "He must have wrapped it around her head ten times and tied it off with a separate knot each time."

"I'm nearly finished here and then I can help you. There! Are you okay, Aunt Ruth?"

"I think so, now that I can breathe again. You and Patrick get Amanda freed and then see if you can open a window for some fresh air. I can smell that nasty dead man and his cheap cologne. I'll feel better when we're out of here and I can get my circulation going again."

Tim helped Patrick with Mrs. Musgrove's gag until it unwound from her face. "It's coming apart now, but he tied your hands and feet with clothes line. Patrick, go in the kitchen and see if you can find a sharp knife in one of the drawers."

"No!" Ruth shouted so loudly that everyone jumped. "There's nothing in the kitchen, Patrick. Don't go in there. It's empty. I already checked it out earlier." She didn't want Patrick anywhere near the kitchen. He might find Darryl's severed head in the refrigerator "Run back to the restaurant and ask Arturo for a couple of sharp knives. And call the police while you're there. We don't need to worry about this scoundrel on the floor, but they have to get here before the Molino brothers come back so they can arrest them."

Patrick flew down the stairs two steps at a time while Tim loosened Amanda Musgrove's scarf from her mouth enough that she could speak, but her words came out in a whisper. "Thank you, Tim."

"Are you going to be alright, Mrs. Musgrove?"

"Perhaps, as your aunt suggested, you could open a window, dear boy. And a glass of water would be nice, as well."

Tim forced both bedroom windows open as far as he could and then ran down the hallway to the kitchen. The double sinks were piled high with pots and pans, stained coffee cups and mismatched flatware covered in caked-on food and dust. Tim found a stack of Styrofoam cups in a cupboard and turned on the cold water tap. It ran brackish at first, but turned clear by the time Tim had searched the drawers and found a serrated steak knife. He carried it with two cups of cold water to the room where his aunt and Nick's grandmother waited.

"Why did you send Patrick to the restaurant, Aunt Ruth?" Tim asked. "I found a steak knife in the kitchen and there were others." He gave each of the women a few sips of water and then started sawing at the ropes that held Mrs. Musgrove's wrists.

"I didn't want to take a chance on him opening the freezer. If he found his friend Darryl's head in there, he might never get the image out of his mind. I only saw photographs of it— not to mention the frozen nose and the eyeball that were in that box in my kitchen—and I'm sure I'll have nightmares. It's bad enough that we all have to see O'Sullivan like this."

Tim stopped what he was doing long enough to open the closet and find an old sheet to spread over the policeman's eyeless face and upper body. Bartholomew leapt out of the darkness, howled and jumped up into Ruth's lap. "There you are, my bad runaway boy," Ruth said. "I can't pet you until my hands are untied, but when we get home I'll make it up to you. And you'll have your front room back. You can spend sunny afternoons in your favorite window without Dianne there to bother you."

"Where is Dianne?" Tim asked. "When we heard three shots, I was sure one of them was meant for her."

"Dianne was the one who fired those shots, young man," Amanda said. "She fired all three shots into our captor here."

"How did he capture you, Amanda?" Ruth asked. "I didn't even know you were in town, but I suspected something when I saw the *Watchtower* stuck in the gate. Why didn't you call me before you came over here all by yourself?"

"I tried calling you from downtown, but I couldn't get through. When I tried again you didn't answer. Then I looked for you at the restaurant and they told me you hadn't been in today. I thought I'd just come back here and have a look around. I saw your cat out in front of this building and followed him in from the street all the way to that room in back where we found him hiding last time. That was where those three men got me cornered."

"O'Sullivan and the Molino brothers?" Tim asked.

"Exactly! It took all three of them to drag me kicking and screaming up to the top floor. They stopped on the stairs to gag me with my own scarf before anyone could hear. After they tied me to the chair, the brothers left me alone with this so-called policeman until Ruth came along and then Dianne."

"Wow!" Tim said. "Do you have any idea where the brothers are now?"

"They said they had some business to take care of, but they threatened to come back before dark to dispose of me," Amanda said. "They talked about how easy it would be for an old lady like me to have some kind of an accident."

"Oh my God!" Ruth said. "Hurry, Tim! What if they come back before the police get here? I mean the real police this time, not this crooked dead one."

"Be quiet a second," Tim whispered. "I think I hear someone." He had finally released Mrs. Musgrove's hands and she was trying to untie her own feet. Tim stepped over the dead man and stood behind the bedroom door with the knife raised over his head, but the voices grew louder and he recognized them. Patrick and Scott barged through the door, followed by Artie who was panting up the stairs behind the two younger men. All three of them carried large knives.

"Who's minding the store?" Ruth asked as Artie and Scott made quick work of cutting off the last of her bonds.

"James is setting up for dinner and Jake should be along soon," Artie said. "There weren't any customers at the bar, anyway. If anyone comes in before we get back they'll just have to wait."

"Can you both walk?" Tim asked the ladies as Scott and Patrick helped them to their feet.

"I think so," Ruth said.

"I think we'll have to," Amanda Musgrove agreed. "Let's get out of here and leave this dead man to the legitimate police."

They stepped over and around the body of Captain O'Sullivan as they filed out of the crowded confines of the room. Sirens grew louder as they descended the stairs. By the time they reached the gate three police cars and an ambulance pulled up in front of the building.

Peter Parker was the first officer to step out of the leading car. Ruth stopped him. "Peter, if you want to catch the Molino brothers, I suggest you get these police cars out of sight or you'll scare them away. Amanda heard them say they'd be back before dark. You might have to wait a while, but your best chance of nabbing them would be by hiding inside, don't you think?"

"We've already got them in custody, Miss Taylor," Peter announced. "We nailed them at their new meth lab down by China Basin. They won't bother you or anyone else for a long time."

"Well, I don't think we'll need the ambulance, young man," Amanda Musgrove said to Peter. She turned toward the paramedics and added, "There's someone on the top floor who is far beyond any help you could give him, but that stretcher might come in handy."

"Peter," Ruth said. "It's Captain O'Sullivan. Dianne shot him before he could tie her up, too. He was involved with the Molino brothers and their drug business all along."

Peter stepped back as if he'd been punched with a hard blow to the stomach. "I had no idea."

"I never thought you did for a minute," Ruth said. She looked around to make sure that Artie, Scott, and especially Patrick were out of earshot before she went on. They'd all headed back to the restaurant. "You see those refrigerators on the sidewalk? They match the one in the photograph that was sent to my apartment. It's in the kitchen on the top floor. I didn't have the nerve to look inside, but one of your people will have to."

"I understand," Peter said. "We'll take care of it."

"We'll be at the bar," Amanda Musgrove announced. "I'm sure you'll have questions for all of us when you're finished with your work here, but in the meanwhile I, for one, could certainly use a stiff drink."

Ruth took Amanda by the arm and said, "I'm sure Artie won't mind if I step behind the bar and make you one of my delicious Rye Manhattans."

As Tim and Ruth and Amanda came in from the back through the kitchen, Arturo arrived through the front door of Arts. "What in the world is going on today?"

"Long story, dear. Did you come here straight from home?" Artie asked.

Arturo nodded. "When I saw Dianne, I knew something must be up. I didn't know she was out of the hospital until I saw her tossing her suitcases and hatboxes into the trunk of that big town car like she was in a race of some kind. She even got the new boys from the second floor apartment to help her out. I thought she was supposed to be sick, but I've never seen a sick person move so fast. Teresa and I just stood there and watched and shook our heads. Then Dianne drove off and she didn't even say good-bye."

"She barely had time to say good-bye to me, Arturo," Ruth said. "But she did put three bullets through our captor. I guess that was her way of saying thank you or good-bye or something. I still can't believe I raised that girl from a newborn and she turned out the way she is. And as much as I hate guns, I have to admit... well... who knew she'd be carrying one in her purse?"

Artie put an arm around Ruth's shoulder and said, "It takes all kinds, you know... it takes all kinds."

Later that evening, after a dinner of Arturo's pot roast, Nick leaned across the table and took Tim's hand. "Well, Snowman, I guess Fleur de Lys will have to wait again, but I don't mind if you don't."

"Hey, this is a step up from our midnight breakfasts at Orphan Andy's, anyway. At least we could get a drink and a bottle of decent wine here, and Sam's paying for the wine. He must be in a very good mood. You can take me someplace expensive another time."

Ruth insisted that she and Sam sit at a table where she could keep an eye on the bar, just in case Artie needed any help. He insisted that his back was fine and not to worry, but the place was filling up and he was busy. "I'm not sure that Artie is ready to be back at work full time," she told Sam. "And where's Scott? He was here earlier."

"I'm sure Artie will let someone know if he needs anything, dear. Relax. Here's Scott now. He must have been in the office." Sam leaned across the table and took Ruth's hand in his. Then he looked into her eyes and smiled. "Meanwhile... I wondered if you'd do something for me, my darling Ruth." He slipped a ring on her finger and watched as her eyes lit up and sparkled along with the diamonds. "Marry me?"

"Oh, Sam... of course I will." Ruth grinned and they both leaned all the way forward across the table for a kiss. "I'd be honored to be your wife."

"There's just one thing you need to know, though..."

"What's that?"

"Well, with the truth about Dianne coming to light, your family has grown a bit smaller while mine is somewhat larger than you've been led to believe. Besides Jane and Ben and the grandkids, I also have—"

"A son?" Ruth interrupted.

"How did you guess?"

"I should have figured it out when we met Adam in the airport in Paris last winter. The way you two greeted each other was so sweet, far more than like old friends. And he's so handsome… just like his father."

Sam squeezed Ruth's hand, but she didn't pause long enough to let him speak. "…and then, the other day, when I was on the phone with Cindy in Boston… Dianne's birth mother…"

"Yes?"

Ruth took a sip of her Martini. "You know, Sam… I don't have a psychic bone in my body. Tim inherited all of that from my mother… his grandmother… but sometimes I can figure things out and I just have to chalk it up to women's intuition, I guess."

"Yes?" Sam sat back in his chair, but kept hold of one of Ruth's hands while she went on. "My old friend Cindy has a son named Adam, too. I was lost in thought and doodling on a slip of paper while we talked on the phone and it came to me again, almost subconsciously. I wrote down the name Adam, along with the names of her other children and just about everyone else's name I could think of… though I wasn't really *thinking*, you know… just doodling… and then those moments at the airport in Paris came back to me and I realized that *your* Adam… simply had to be…"

"Ruth, I want you to know that Delia… Adam's mother… and I were only together that one time. It was just after my wife died. Delia had always run the house and she was a great comfort to me, especially then, but our relationship was never a romantic one. I would say that night was all a big mistake, but I've never regretted having Adam as a son. Delia married

Frank within a year after he was born. Adam was still in diapers when they met and—"

"Sam," Ruth interrupted, "you don't need to explain a thing to me. I'm looking forward to getting to know Adam better, and Alexandra, too. He and Tim will be almost like cousins and I think that's wonderful."

"And you'll be in charge of that house from now on, Ruth… once we're married, you'll be the queen of the manor."

"Now, let's not get ahead of ourselves. I said I'd marry you, but I wouldn't think of getting in Delia's way. She does a fine job and I have no desire to take over as the head of housekeeping." Ruth laughed. "I wouldn't mind making dinner for the two of us now and then, but no more than maybe once a week. Between Delia and Arturo I might even learn how to cook fish. But there'll be plenty of time to talk about all that later."

"Plenty of time," Sam agreed.

"And *please,* Sam… don't call me the *queen* of anything. We have plenty of queens around here as it is, and I wouldn't want to get in the way of any of them, either."

Sam and Ruth both had a laugh and looked around the restaurant. The only one who wasn't happy at the moment was Teresa. As the others sat down to eat, she stayed at the bar, ordered her fourth Martini from Scott and complained, "Gay men, married men, police men… they're all the same—no good!"

"What happened to Peter Parker?" Artie asked.

Ruth looked up from the table and said, "I thought you two were getting along so well. Don't get discouraged. Every relationship has its ups and downs, you know."

"Just like the bathroom scale," Artie added. "Except in my case it's been all ups lately. I've gained twelve pounds since last Christmas and it's all because I threw my back out. I'll never get back in my old gowns by Pride Week at this rate! All I want to do when I'm on Vicodin is eat!"

"Did you and Officer Parker have a falling-out, dear?" Ruth asked.

"No, not exactly… not at all! But he told me he wouldn't be coming by later—not tonight, not tomorrow, not next week. He's moving away! He's taking a job with a private security firm in Vegas. It's a big increase in salary and he can be closer to his ex-wife and kids. Who knew he had kids? His little boy smashed up his bicycle today and broke his leg in two places. He'll be alright, but Peter was so upset he's flying down there tonight!"

"I'm so sorry, Teresa," Ruth said.

Scott had already chilled a fresh stemmed glass. Now he scooped ice into the shaker to make Teresa another drink, "He sounds like a good daddy, anyway."

"That one's on the house, Scott" Artie reached over and patted Teresa's free hand.

"I'm giving up men, I swear! They're more trouble than they're worth! I should have been a lesbian all along. I'll bet I'd make a good one, don't ya think? Don't be skimpy with the gin there, Scotty old boy…"

It was well past midnight when Nick and Tim curled up together in Tim's bed on Hancock Street. They were just about to drift off to sleep when more sirens wailed through the neighborhood.

Tim remembered his dream from the other night and realized that this must be the fire he saw in it. Some of his dreams were only dreams. Others recalled an important event from his past, but in this case his dream had predicted the future. As impressive as this fire was, it was also cleansing. It left a black gap in that block of Hartford Street where a new building would soon take its place. And it helped erase the horror of the scene where Patrick's friend Darryl met his death and where Tim's Aunt Ruth and Nick's grandmother nearly met theirs. Tim didn't care so much about what happened to his cousin Dianne, even though he had to admit she'd saved the day.

Some of the crowd on Castro Street that night, those who were moving from bar to bar, witnessed the fire engines come from all directions and then head east, both on 18th and 19th Streets. The red ambulances and the hook and ladder trucks turned onto Hartford Street from both ends and met in the middle. No one ever knew what started the fire and nothing much was left to investigate afterward. Volatile chemicals had seeped into the floors, ensuring that the old wooden building behind Arts went up like a torch. There was little the firemen could do but concentrate their efforts on keeping the restaurant safe and hosing down the houses on either side, especially the one that was only inches away.

"You know something? Tim asked. "Sometimes I get tired of listening to all these sirens. You must hardly ever hear them in Monte Rio, I'll bet."

"Only when you're around, Snowman," Nick answered sleepily, pressing his lips to the back of Tim's ear and flicking at the lobe with his tongue. "When you're around I hear sirens and fireworks and sometimes violins... and I feel earthquakes all the time."

Tim let out a satisfied moan and shrugged his shoulders. "I was thinking a while back about taking a long drive down the coast. I thought I might even go as far as L.A. and look up some old friends of Jason's down there... or maybe not. Maybe I'll just keep driving until I get tired of it. Stop when I feel like it, rest a while."

"That sounds nice."

"Wanna come with me?"

"I've got about three weeks before I need to get started on that new winery project."

"We could take turns driving and there are some great beaches all along the way."

"We can get lots of sun and eat steaks and tons of fresh seafood and at night we could check into one of those little seaside cabins or sleep in motel rooms with beds where you drop a quarter into the slot and get the magic fingers and—"

"I'll show you some magic fingers, stud," Tim said, laughing. "Do you mean it? Can you really come with me? I was going to forget the whole thing, but I've been thinking about starting back to work at Arts in a couple of weeks and it would be great to get out of town first. If you could come with me it would really be fun."

"I'll go anywhere with you, Snowman. We could keep right on driving all the way down the coast to Mexico. You could stretch two weeks into three and I could stretch three weeks into four, but then I really have to get back to work. How does a month sound? We haven't had a honeymoon in a long time."

"Mmmm..." Tim moaned. "Sounds good to me."

# A sneak peek at Chapter 1

# from

# Mark Abramson's

# Wedding Season

Book 5 of the Beach Reading series

The ceremony was about to start when Tim Snow looked around and saw dozens, maybe hundreds of smiling faces. He knew every one of them and all of them were dressed to the nines. Organ music groaned through the sanctified air and crescendoed like waves of a crashing sea. He thought he must be inside the Castro Theatre. They have a massive pipe organ there, but no center aisle for a bride to enter on the arm of her father and stroll out on the arm of her new husband. And the lighting was too bright for the Castro Theatre. Sunlight sent yellow shafts through stained glass windows lighting the faces of women in flowered hats. Most of the men wore suits and ties. Tim had been looking forward to this day for a long time, his Aunt Ruth's wedding to Sam Connor.

The music changed, the organ stop was reset to sound a one-note trumpet fanfare and a lone bridesmaid appeared in the aisle. The room was so cavernous that Tim wondered if this was Grace Cathedral. Now he watched from the front where he stood beside Sam's son Adam, the handsome black fashion model from Chicago.

The bridesmaid limped a few steps closer and staggered. She grabbed the arm of a pew and tried to right herself, but reeled and fell. A middle-aged man in a blue suit stood and tried to help her, but she spat at him and pushed him away. Tim recognized his own mother, blind drunk, but he was as helpless as anyone else. She dropped her bouquet and crawled toward the altar, drooling like a rabid dog. Her foot caught on the flowers, tearing them apart and leaving a trail of petals down the aisle.

Tim turned red with rage. Everyone must wonder why this pathetic woman was there. Someone would figure out that the bride, Ruth Taylor, only had one sister and therefore, since Ruth was Tim's aunt that could only mean the woman must be… Tim would never admit it! He would deny that he knew her, that he'd ever laid eyes on her before!

Now he turned his anger toward his Aunt Ruth, who hadn't yet appeared. She should have known better. She should have warned Tim that his mother was invited. She should have known full well how her drunken sister would make a fool of herself and ruin an otherwise perfect day.

"Hey! Wake up, Tim, are you okay, babe?" It was Nick looking down at him, shaking him.

"Yeah, I'm fine. It's just a dream. No big deal." Tim felt Nick's arm wrap around him as he lay back down, strong and warm and comforting as ever and soon they were both asleep again.

Now he watched the scene from above. The organ music still played, but Tim's mother was gone and it was peaceful again. Waves lapped at a nearby shore and Tim could hear seagulls and a distant foghorn. Maybe this was Adam's wedding to Alexandra, but there was no ocean in Chicago. The organ's notes turned into the sound of the sea again and they faded away this time. Now the congregation was dressed in pastels. Men and women wore big flowered hats. Now he understood. Many of the men were in drag.

It was a wedding alright, but it was taking place in Arts restaurant on Castro Street. The place was ten times bigger in Tim's dream than in reality. Phil was playing the piano, naked—there was no pipe organ if you didn't count the massive organ between Phil's legs. He wasn't completely naked, either. He had on that silly bow-tie he wore on special occasions with starched cuffs and silver cufflinks and probably black patent leather shoes, although Tim couldn't see Phil's feet. Tim moaned again and felt Nick touching him, shaking him until he came to.

"Huh?" Tim blinked. "Where am I? What's going on?"

"You're right here safe beside me, Snowman. You were just having another dream."

Tim was used to wild dreams. They were a common side-effect of the HIV drugs he took every day. He didn't mind the dreams, as long as the drugs kept working, keeping his viral load undetectable and his T-cells over 500 at last count. Most people had lots worse things than dreams to worry about, whether they had HIV or not. Tim knew there were lots worse things than HIV, too.

"Oh, Nick, did I wake you up? I'm sorry. What time is it, anyway?"

"It's almost 7:30, time to get up. I was awake, anyway. It's time to pack up and head home pretty soon. You were mumbling about a wedding and then you mentioned Phil and then something about an earthquake. I thought I'd better try to wake you 'cause you don't usually talk in your sleep. Are you sure you're okay?"

"Thanks." Tim sat up and rubbed his eyes. "Yeah... I'm okay. It wasn't such a bad dream except the part when my mother was shit-faced and ruining Aunt Ruth's wedding. I don't remember any earthquake. The whole thing was so weird and then I wasn't sure who was getting married. It might have been someone else. There were all these drag queens at Arts in big hats like Easter bonnets and lots of other people. I knew most of them."

"Maybe we should take a run on the beach. It might clear your head and we could work up an appetite for breakfast before we head back to the city."

"Head back...? What beach? Is that the ocean I hear? I thought I was listening to a pipe organ. Where are we?"

"Don't you remember?" Nick lifted the palm of his hand to Tim's forehead. "It doesn't feel like you have a fever, but maybe you're a little warm. We're in a cabin south of Carmel.

We were driving back up the coast from L.A., just taking our time and you said you wanted to stop here and spend our last night on the road. Don't you remember? We were planning to be back in San Francisco by this afternoon or this evening, but it doesn't matter to me. If you're not feeling well, we can stay here longer… at least until you feel better."

"Oh, sure I remember. I'm feeling okay now. Don't worry. It was just a dream."

"So… you were dreaming about a wedding, huh? Do you think it might have been *our* wedding? Yours and mine?

"I thought it was Sam and Ruth getting married," Tim said, ignoring Nick's attempt to get closer to him, "but it could have been anybody, I suppose. At first I thought it was in the Castro Theatre, but then I realized it was broad daylight and it would have been dark in there. Then it seemed like it was in some huge, cavernous place like Grace Cathedral or maybe St. Mary's or that big white one in Minneapolis just north of Loring Park."

"I think I detect a change of subject, young man," Nick said. "I was asking about you and me, but maybe you'd like to go have a run on the beach and we can talk about it later."

"Now I remember where we are. I remember last night and the night before and that place we pulled over in the car above the ocean and watched the sunset… You know, Nick, sometimes I think you and I do honeymoons so well that we should just stick to what we're good at. Why do we need to talk about getting married?"

"You remember all that, do you?" Nick asked and slid in closer, putting his arm around Tim's shoulders.

"Yes, I do remember now and I can think of a better way to work up an appetite for breakfast than running." Tim pushed Nick back down on the bed. He kicked off the covers and climbed on top of him, straddling his chest and then leaning in close to nuzzle his neck and kiss him on the mouth. "Does it make me a top if I sit on it?"

"I'm not into labels," Nick laughed. "You can be whatever you want, Snowman… just don't stop."

...

By the time they opened the door of the cabin the sun was high in the sky. They pulled on shorts and went for a barefoot run on the sandy beach together and than took showers and finished packing. Check-out time was posted at 10AM but there was no one else around when they were ready to go. Tim dropped their room key through the mail slot of the locked office door. Maybe the proprietors were off on an errand.

They pulled over once to put the top up on the car because a bank of white fog was piling in over the city. By the time they got home it would be cold enough to light a fire in the fireplace in Tim's living room on Hancock Street tonight. Nick took a turn behind the wheel of Tim's Thunderbird as they headed up California's Highway 1 toward Pacifica. Nick was happier than he'd been in a long time and he knew better than to press Tim again about any further commitments. Tim was right. They were very good at honeymoons. Weddings could wait.

To Be Continued...

## About the Author

Born and raised a Minnesota farm-boy, Mark Abramson has lived in San Francisco so long he is now a native. Not only did he survive the worst of the AIDS years in California, but also the Reagan era AND both Bush administrations. He is thrilled that the *Beach Reading* series, his first foray into fiction, has been so successful and he is grateful to the loyal fans of Tim, Aunt Ruth, Artie and the rest of the gang. For Mark, it's easier to make up stories about the Castro because no one would believe all of the true ones!